Officer Barcomb

VS

The Undead

Darren S. Barcomb

Slaughterhouse Press

Plattsburgh, New York

ISBN: 9781973427254

Dedication

Thanks go out to Mom and Dad for a lifetime of support, to Debbie for continued motivation, and the Brothers of Nu Chapter of Theta Gamma for always having my back.

Chapter 1: Boots on the Ground

"If he moves, you take his fuckin' head off."

The van barreled down the off-ramp into The Burg and Barcomb swung it onto East Jersey.

"You fuckin' hear me?" Barcomb said. "Take no chances. If he even thinks about going for a piece, you bury that son of a bitch."

The red lights lit up liquor stores, strip joints and vacant lots as Barcomb hit Berkman Street and headed deeper into The Burg, the bank robbery capital of New Jersey and the jewel in the crown of the drug-trafficking trade in the city of Elizabeth. It was quiet for ten p.m., but a few beat-up husbands in beat-up cars drove around looking for beat-up call girls. Barcomb hammered through traffic and it scattered as the siren screamed all the way into Concord Avenue.

"How many we expecting?" Reyes said, shouting over the roar of the engine.

"No more than we can handle," Barcomb said. He glanced at Reyes beside him and then into the rear-view at Munday. He didn't like what he saw. Randy Reyes was twenty-four years old and had as much experience on the street as anyone his age - not very much - but there was something about him none of the guys liked, a softness. It was hard to pin down. He was too quick to smile, too slow to anger; his voice was quiet and his tone apologetic. First guy he shot, he sent flowers to his wife. The perp wasn't even dead. Reyes was just that kind of guy. Everyone could see that he was living on borrowed time. Sooner or later, the street would get him killed. The only person who didn't know it was him.

"How far?" Munday shouted.

"Three minutes," Barcomb said.

As Barcomb drove, Munday adjusted her vest. Two months on the job and it had never fit her right. They each wore tactical and bulletproof vests and were dressed in black with only the glint of their cuffs and two patches of white to distinguish them from the shadows: the word "POLICE" and a monochrome stars-and-stripes. Rachel Munday had forgotten her gloves and the cold air rushing through the window made her restless. Barcomb knew these two wouldn't be enough, but they were off-book now and these two were just chicken shit enough not to tell anyone while still being dumb enough to come along.

Barcomb killed the lights and the siren as they hit the corner of Liberty and Exeter. He slowed and Reyes and Munday fell silent.

"Where is everyone?" Barcomb said.

The street was empty. Cars were parked on the side of the road with their lights left on and their doors left wide open. The bass of *You've Got Another Thing Coming* pounded from a run-down sports bar and through the windows Barcomb caught a glimpse of a dozen people thrashing at each other and throwing glasses. Not my problem, he thought. The Devils and the Rangers were playing up in Newark and that always meant trouble.

It's why he chose tonight.

Barcomb thought he heard a scream from the bar.

Must be a good game, he thought. But ice hockey wasn't really his sport. Barcomb demanded a little more contact, a little more blood and sweat. He had to grow up fast when he was a kid, learn to take

2

punches as well as he could give them, and it gave him a respect for the fight. He brought that to his work. Some guys said he was a little out of touch - that rough stuff was outdated, they said - but for him it was about respect. Some cops try worming their way in, becoming pals and earning respect that way; "I'm just a regular guy, like you," was their play. Barcomb didn't want any more pals. Barcomb wasn't a regular guy. If someone didn't have respect for Barcomb, he'd beat it into them.

The bars gave way to the projects as Barcomb went further into The Burg. He caught glimpses of people running in the dark spaces between houses. Their black Chevy Suburban was unmarked, but the lookouts all knew it. Police activity in the projects had been kept to a minimum while the latest trial was underway, but Barcomb had busted enough skulls around here to make them remember. Barcomb turned into Atlantic Street and couldn't hear a thing. Not even the dogs were barking.

They know to stay out of my way, he thought.

Barcomb's phone rang.

"I can't stay here," whispered the woman's voice on the other end.

"Is he there? Rhona, is he fucking there?" Barcomb said.

"Something's wrong," Rhona replied. "I think they've seen me."

"Is Dutroux still inside?"

"I haven't seen him for a while, but he went in. Listen, please. Something is really fucked up. I don't know what it-"

The line went dead.

3

"What she say?" Munday inquired.

Reyes wiped the sweat from his forehead. "We on?"

Barcomb frowned and nodded. "Dutroux's in there," he said. "We're on."

Barcomb stopped under an off-ramp next to an empty homeless camp site. Five torn-up tents swayed in the breeze. The fire was still smoking. The piss against the wall was still wet. There was no-one around. The Burg was usually full of activity, a wasps' nest of crack heads, hookers and half-starved kids on BMX bikes. It troubled Barcomb. He couldn't shake the feeling that he was walking into something bad.

Focus, he thought.

He laid it out for Munday and Reyes. "You can still go home," he said. "No-one knows you're here and no-one will ever know you got this far. You do this, however, and no-one can ever know that either. We get this fuck. You shut your mouth. That's it. Everyone sleeps better. I hear a word of this on the street, you better sleep with your fucking eyes open. You get me? So, what? You guys in?"

"I can't live knowing Dutroux is out there, walking around like everyone else," Munday said. "Not after what he did."

Barcomb looked at Reyes. "What he did, is it enough for you? The money will be there. The dope will be there. We can take him in," Barcomb said, "but I aim for this to go wrong. This isn't gonna end well for him. He doesn't get to walk away. We write this up afterwards as a drug bust gone wrong. Not a word out of line. Anyone's there we don't like, they go too."

Reyes nodded.

"If he moves, take him out. If he doesn't, you leave him for me. Whatever happens. Listen to me, Reyes. Munday, you clear? Whatever happens, this motherfucker doesn't get to walk away," Barcomb said.

They got out of the car and Barcomb pulled his Glock.

They pulled on their ski masks.

*

Officer Darren Barcomb had been haunting the streets of Elizabeth with a gun and a badge for over ten years — six on patrol, paying his dues, and now four on the strike team — but he had never seen it so quiet.

It was a small city, but Elizabeth was at the heart of Union County and home to many of the criminals operating out of Newark on the other side of the airport and in Jersey City across the bay. The backyard of Elizabeth was the refinery and the port, both making up the backbone of the city and keeping its people on the right side of surviving. When the refinery closed, the sharks from Newark and Jersey City moved in. James Dutroux was one such shark, his coming announced by the bloated, blue bodies of his competitors floating in the Arthur Kill, the strait separating Elizabeth from Staten Island. Elizabeth P.D. took the fight to Dutroux for years, but it led to nothing but chump-change jail terms for his lieutenants and Dutroux buying off half the police force.

When one of Dutroux's dirty cops turned and gave up half the force in the biggest Internal Affairs operations in the department's history, it was only a matter of time until Dutroux found him.

Dutroux mailed the officer's head to Internal Affairs in a box.

Barcomb made himself remember seeing his partner's head in that box. He needed the rage. He could feel it taking hold of him, controlling him, making him sharper, stronger. His black-gloved hands shook as he crept around the back of the six-story tenement, the infamous Reilly-Russell apartments known by the locals as "Hell House". Barcomb saw the white eyes of the enormous face of the graffiti devil which had watched from the wall for over ten years, covering half of the six stories, its lower jaw covered in gang tags and names in faded spray paint.

The eyes watched him.

The ground beneath Barcomb's feet was soft, almost shifting. He stopped behind a rusted out Honda Accord with no wheels. He put his back to it and listened. He could feel his warm breath inside the ski mask. Munday and Reyes were close behind. There was no sign of Barcomb's informant, Rhona.

"Where's the snitch?" Munday asked.

"I don't see her," Barcomb said. "Must've booked out of here."

Reyes looked around frantically, his eyes almost tearing up. "Something's really crazy here," he said. "Can you guys feel that?"

Munday and Barcomb looked at each other.

"The ground," Barcomb said. "It's moving."

"What the fuck is it?" Munday asked.

"Who cares? Hold it together," Barcomb said. "I don't see a lookout. We're heading up. I want the money in the room when we head in there. It needs to look good."

"That must be the seller's car," Munday said, pointing to a Ford sedan much too shiny to be local. Its doors were all open and its interior lights were on, but no-one was around. "I don't like it. Where is everyone?"

Barcomb felt the ground push up against the underside of his boot. He put it to the back of his mind. He only had room for what he needed to do. "Let's find out," Barcomb said, moving out from behind the car.

*

Hell House lived up to its reputation. Barcomb, Reyes and Munday forced an entry through a rear fire exit between graffiti of a nun with fire for eyes and pastel-colored children's hand-prints, presumably left over from a kindergarten class from the nearby Pitarra Elementary, which the kids all named "The Pits" on account of its status as one of the most crime-ridden schools in the state of New Jersey. If knife crimes were football wins, Barcomb had always said, The Pits would have a hell of a trophy cabinet. The stench inside the tenement was overwhelming and the darkness was near-total.

Munday wrapped a handkerchief around her face to cover her nose and mouth. She whispered, "What in Christ's name have they been doing down here?" Barcomb took out a flashlight and held it up beside the barrel of his Glock, walking with slow, deliberate steps. They made it into the stairwell and Munday stepped in something. She tried scraping it off on the stairs.

7

"Dog shit," Munday cursed.

"You wish," Barcomb said.

The stairs were stained with piss. Broken syringes cracked under their boots. They stopped at every floor level and listened.

Nothing.

Munday mouthed to Barcomb, "Why is it so quiet?"

Barcomb didn't answer. He pointed up towards the top floor. They had things to be doing.

The sixth floor smelled the worst, like something had crawled inside, died and shit all over itself in the process. A strip light in the corridor buzzed and blinked as it hung from its fixture. Barcomb pointed to the door at the end of the hall. Munday and Reyes nodded and went ahead. Barcomb moved slowly behind them, his Glock drawn, listening as he passed each door. He heard TV game shows, the low moaning of life-changing sex, and a crying baby, but the loudest sound was his own footsteps. The state had put everything into locking Dutroux down over and over again, but it always fell apart. Years of work lost through a couple of procedural errors exploited by a lawyer who got paid more in a week than Barcomb did all year. This last trial was going south already. He can't get away again, Barcomb thought.

This was Barcomb's only shot at something like justice.

He knew he couldn't fuck it up.

Dutroux's door had a wrought-iron screen with a chair outside, probably for a bodyguard. Barcomb couldn't help but be disappointed that

Dutroux was so small time, operating out of a shit hole like this. The guy ran around Elizabeth like he owned the place and this was his set up?

The chair was empty.

The door was open.

Blood pooled on the carpet, darkening the welcome mat which read "Fuck off!" Munday and Reyes took a side of the door each. Barcomb walked up to the center. He lowered his weapon to his hip, still ready to fire, and pulled the door open with his free hand.

Barcomb could hear the TV, local news anchors squawking about a riot over in Newark, and he could hear movement. Someone was shuffling around.

Barcomb clicked his fingers at Reyes and pointed to a side bedroom. He nodded to Munday and gestured towards the lounge, mouthing "Follow me."

The blood pooled at the door formed a red path to the lounge. The door was shut. Barcomb tried it quietly, but something blocked it on the other side. He put his ear to the door and listened. The shuffling stopped.

Barcomb waited.

Suddenly, Reyes shouted from the other room: "Barcomb! Shit! Oh, fuck!"

Barcomb pulled the trigger in his mind in less than a second. He turned and pointed for Munday to see to Reyes and, turning back without breaking momentum, he kicked the lounge door down on his own in one motion and was inside, weapon drawn.

It was a slaughterhouse.

Blood dripped from the ceiling fan. The floor was a motionless carpet of human beings in different states of being torn apart. Limbs and intestines were ripped and scattered from their owners to such an extent that Barcomb couldn't tell how many people he was looking at. He instinctively scanned the room for weapons and saw handguns and shotguns lying all around, but the corpses had not been shot; they had been shredded. It looked as if a pack of rabid wolves had been let loose in the place. There was no sense to be made of the scene. There was only carnage.

"Barcomb!" Munday shouted. She pulled Reyes in, taking his weight on her shoulders. "Some fuckin' maniac bit his neck!"

"He down?" Barcomb asked.

"Got him."

Reyes's eyes begged for help as he drowned in his own blood. His windpipe stuck through the gash on his throat and the wound bled into the opening. He collapsed on the floor. Barcomb had seen death, but very little first hand and up close as it happened. Good cops save lives; that's what he always believed. At least until Dutroux put his partner's head in a box and called down the wrath of god. Barcomb could see Reyes slipping away. He coughed and spluttered and looked like he couldn't believe it was happening.

"Put pressure on that," Barcomb said. "I need to secure the rest of the apartment."

Munday pushed down on Reyes's neck and blood sprayed up into her face, darkening her blonde hair, dripping from her ponytail. She spat it out of her mouth as she held on. "Don't you die," she said. "Winners don't die."

10

Barcomb kicked at the more complete corpses on the floor to look for survivors, ignoring those which had been torn completely apart. He saw the bathroom door was closed and tried the handle.

Locked.

A clattering and a sobbing sound came from inside.

"Come out of there, right now!" Barcomb shouted. "Elizabeth P.D.! Get your ass out!"

"Oh, thank god! Don't shoot!" a voice came. "Don't fuckin' shoot!" The door opened slowly.

"Hands where I can see them!"

A silver-plated Desert Eagle was tossed out of the bathroom door shortly before a pair of blood-soaked hands appeared. Munday pushed Reyes's eyes closed and stood up. She drew her weapon and trained it on the bathroom door.

"I thought you guys would never show the fuck up, man." The man in the bathroom walked out with his hands held high. He wore an open red Hawaiian shirt and was bare-chested underneath; he had on a pair of white shorts, now red, and sandals. He was black, round-bellied and in his mid-30s with a long, wiry beard and the number 23 shaved into his hair. He had a big smile for Munday. "Damn, girl," he said. "I didn't phone no stripper gram, but I'll take one."

His smile disappeared when he saw Barcomb. "Hello, Dutroux," Barcomb said

"Barcomb?"

"Someone's coming," Munday said, spinning to face the other door.

"Look, Barcomb, man," Dutroux said. "We gotta get outta this fuckin' joint right fuckin' now. I know we got some shit, but there is some fucked up shit going on tonight. I can't even-"

"Shut the fuck up," Munday said. "Listen."

Distant shrieking carried through the building's corridors, distant howls and distant moans.

"What the fuck is that?" Barcomb said.

"We gotta leave, man." Dutroux said. "They on some crazy shit. I ain't even kidding. Motherfuckers come in here and start tearing shit up and they don't go down, you know?"

Barcomb looked at Dutroux as the noises grew louder and closer.

"They don't go down," Dutroux repeated.

The door to the apartment splintered into pieces and a blood-drenched man stood in the doorway, looking around as if sniffing for food. Barcomb approached. "Down on the ground!" he shouted. "Get those fucking hands behind your head and kiss the floor."

The man tilted his head like a curious dog and started running at Barcomb.

"Freeze!" Barcomb shouted. "Freeze right now or I'll be forced to fire!"

"Don't shoot that fuckin' thing!" Dutroux shouted. "You'll bring them here!"

The man was a foot away when Barcomb fired two rounds to the man's chest, sinking him. Barcomb turned to Munday.

"What the fuck is going on, Munday?"

12

At that moment the lull in conversation was filled by noise from the TV set. An attractive female reporter stood outside the Prudential Center, home of the New Jersey Devils in Newark, as thousands upon thousands of people ran screaming from the stadium. She shouted over the noise, but only a few words made it through: "cannibals", "insane", "stay inside". Barcomb, Munday and Dutroux watched as the crowds swept over the reporter and she and the camera were crushed in the panic. The dropped camera froze with an image of her screaming face amid a sea of panicked people's feet stepping on her head and back, crushing her to death.

The dead man in the hallway stood up.

Barcomb turned and looked. "You gotta be fucking kidding me," he said.

He raised his weapon and fired again.

Chest shot.

The man kept coming.

Another shot to the chest didn't drop him. He kept coming.

A gunshot sounded behind Barcomb and the dead man's head exploded, the broken egg shells of his skull embedding into the walls, his brains sliding silently to the floor. Dutroux stood behind Barcomb with his Desert Eagle raised.

"That seems to work," Dutroux said.

Barcomb scowled at him. Down the hall, they could see the stairwell door opening slowly as ravenous, blood-soaked people fought one another to get through. They shrieked and moaned and gasped, all language replaced by hunger and rage.

"You're gonna need my help if you're gonna get out of here alive," Dutroux said.

Reyes lay on the floor with his windpipe torn out of his neck, the blood pooling up around his dead body.

Barcomb looked at Reyes and then back to the on-coming crowd of hysterical maniacs. They clawed at one another to get past. Barcomb had never seen anything like it.

Barcomb, Munday and Dutroux checked their ammo.

Reyes stood up behind them.

Chapter 2: Dead, But Not

"What the holy fuck is going on?" Barcomb said as the hallway was filled with crazy people fighting with one another to get through to the apartment. They didn't punch, he noticed, not like regular people. They clawed and bit each other like rabid dogs. They tore at each other. Barcomb had never seen anything like it. Dutroux's mouth was hanging open in disbelief.

"I knew I should've stayed in Brooklyn," Dutroux said. "Motherfuckers there be crazy, but this is some *other* shit!"

Barcomb moved fast and barricaded the doorway, locking the screen and propping everything up with a set of drawers and a heavy chair. He turned and saw Reyes standing behind Dutroux. Reyes's head was hanging down, limp. Blood still poured from his neck. Dutroux heard the splashing as Reyes's blood hit the floor and he froze. Reyes looked up and bared his teeth. Barcomb looked at Reyes closely. He couldn't see anything of the guy he once knew in there. The eyes still had that dull, matte look, like a corpse or a shark. The eyeballs didn't move; the entire head moved instead, making Reyes look almost drunk.

Reyes lunged for Dutroux.

Barcomb shot Reyes through the eye, sending him slamming back down to the floor.

Dutroux took a deep breath.

Reyes lay there bleeding from another part of his body now.

"He was dead," Barcomb said. "Dead as I've ever seen anyone."

"That's what I was sayin', homes," Dutroux said. "They don't go down. These some undead motherfuckers. That headshot seemed to do the fuckin' trick though. Shit."

15

Barcomb pulled up his radio. "Ten-thirty-three over at Reilly-Russell. Ten-thirty-three. Immediate assistance. Officer down. Officer down. You catching me?"

The silence seemed to last forever.

"Ten-thirty-three at Reilly-Russell," Barcomb said. "We're in some real shit over here. Come in."

"Negative, Barcomb," came the response. "We got riots and murders all over the city. There's no-one left to send."

"Say that again," Barcomb said.

"There's not enough cops to go around. You're on your own, Darren. Stay safe."

Barcomb lowered his radio and looked the apartment door. It was starting to give way to the pressure of the undead beyond, the wood buckling and starting to splinter.

"Motherfuckers," Dutroux said.

Munday was over at the window, her hand on her mouth and almost a tear in her eye. She took a breath and said, "Barcomb, you're gonna want to see this."

Barcomb stepped over the slimy intestines and half-eaten faces of Dutroux's men to get to the window. What he saw outside made him mouth the word "Motherfucker."

Elizabeth burned. Her people were tearing each other apart with their bare hands. Some leapt from apartment buildings to their deaths. Some tried to escape in their cars and were bogged down in the undead before being devoured. In the distance, the airport was ablaze. Two airliners met in the sky in an enormous explosion over City Hall and showered Elizabeth with flaming wreckage and the toasted body parts of five hundred or so people.

"The whole world has gone to shit," Barcomb said.

"What are we gonna do?" Munday asked. Dutroux walked over and saw the chaos outside.

Dutroux had nothing to say.

Barcomb looked at Dutroux as he spoke to Munday: "What the fuck do we do with this scumbag, now, do you think?"

"Shit is fucked. You need me, homes," Dutroux said.

Barcomb punched Dutroux in the face, slamming the back of his head against the wall, and took his weapon.

"Come on, man!" Dutroux said, his eyes tearing up and his breathing erratic. "You guys is fucked without me, homes. You're as dead as your friend there!"

Barcomb squinted at him and gritted his teeth. He dropped him to the floor and said, "You're right. I need you." He handed Dutroux his Desert Eagle. "You better hope I keep on needing you for some time, because the second I don't I'm gonna feed you to these crazy bastards."

The door caved and the undead began to pour into the room. They looked different in their general appearance - crack addicts, prostitutes, and a pizza delivery boy - but they all shared that hungry shark look in their eyes. They were different, but the same, like a colony of ants all driven by one purpose: to destroy.

Opening the window, Barcomb swung a leg out and looked down. It was a big drop. He barked orders at Munday: "I'm heading into the room below. I'll clear it while you watch Dutroux. Send him down next, then you. It's a small drop, but we can do it. There's too many up here."

Munday fired a couple of rounds into one of the undead who made it past the barricade, the bullets taking chunks from the person's head until he collapsed in a heap. The sight of blood seemed to make the others even more frenzied.

17

"This is nuts, yo," Dutroux said, looking out the window. "I can't let go and grab that next shit."

"If you don't, it's a long way down."

Barcomb holstered his weapon and stretched his fingers out and back in, looking down at the window ledge below which he had to grab onto.

This isn't exactly how I expected today to go, Barcomb thought.

He took two deep breaths, looked up at Munday unloading her Glock into the swarm of the undead trying to get through the door and realized he didn't have time for a third. He jumped.

He felt the air rush by his face and the felt the impact of the window ledge beneath knock the wind out of him. He grabbed onto the inside of the window frame. It was mercifully open. He felt his grip loosening and scrambled up, pushing his feet against the wall. Within moments he had pulled himself inside and rolled over onto his back and drawn his Glock. The apartment was empty except for a mattress on the floor, a TV on a crate and empty vodka bottles.

"Come on down!" Barcomb shouted up. He stood by the window as Dutroux dangled his legs from above.

"Don't you let me fuckin' drop!" Dutroux shouted. He let go. "Shiiiit!"

Dutroux hit the window ledge chin-first and bounced back. Barcomb grabbed him by his shirt and then his wrist, but Dutroux was too heavy. Dutroux flapped around and squealed.

"Don't you fuckin' let go of me, motherfucker!" he shouted.

Barcomb felt his grip failing as Dutroux's weight was pulling him out of the window. He heard Munday firing upstairs, shouting about ammunition.

"Grab the next ledge!" Barcomb shouted.

"What?!" Dutroux screamed.

"The next ledge down! Fuckin' grab that one, you fat sack of shit! Three, two-"

"Don't you-"

"One!"

Barcomb let go of Dutroux and he fell screaming to the floor below. He hit the window ledge and clung on for his life. He hung there kicking his legs frantically before finally pulling himself up. Barcomb heard glass break and Dutroux disappeared through the window.

Fuck, Barcomb thought. I'm not losing this prick.

"Come on down!" Barcomb shouted at Munday.

A body flew through the air past the window at speed, landing on the concrete below in a huge splash of dark blood. Barcomb felt a surge of instant panic and looked down.

It was one of the undead.

Munday swung her legs down and then dropped. Barcomb caught her and pulled her inside, his hands on her ass, and they both landed on their backs inside the room. She was as firm as she looked, he thought. No wonder the guys at the station all tried to land her.

"You get a good feel?" she said, adjusting her tactical vest.

"Saved your life, didn't I?" Barcomb said. "Let's go find Dutroux. The fat fuck dropped an extra floor."

19

"Maybe you should've grabbed his ass?" Munday said with a smile.

*

The corridors of the fifth floor pounded with the noise of the undead masses upstairs. They screamed and screeched and bounced off the walls as if completely possessed. Barcomb and Munday moved quietly towards the stairwell, their boots squelching in the carpet wet and black with blood.

They must've taken the whole building, Barcomb thought. Where the hell did they all come from?

As if reading his mind, Munday whispered, "They must've all been dead before we even got here."

Barcomb realized something. "The drug buy must've been a trap," he said. "Hell House is owned by Dutroux. All his men and their families live here. The supplier must've been a competitor, taken everyone out during the exchange."

"Taken out everyone?"

"Maybe not, but enough of them must've died to get a couple of these undead fucks up and running. Enough to make sure everyone had a real shitty day."

"Whoever that supplier was, he chose a bad day to stage a massacre."

"Yeah," Barcomb said. "No fuckin' shit."

They moved in and out of the shadows created in the hallway by the broken lighting. Apartment doors had been left open. Barcomb glimpsed broken furniture, bloodied walls, and empty cribs. A scream from the stairwell sent Barcomb and Munday running for it.

Dutroux was pistol-whipping an undead attacker over and over. "Fuck off me!" he screamed, over and over.

Barcomb nailed him with a headshot and Dutroux's mouth was suddenly full of hot brains and sharp skull fragments. He pushed the corpse off and spit everything out, rubbing his tongue on his shirt to get rid of the foul, metallic taste. He scowled at Barcomb.

"You're welcome," Barcomb said.

Their voices echoed in the scum-encrusted stairwell and Barcomb was conscious that the others might follow the sound of the gunshot.

"We better get out of here," Munday said.

"Come on, baby," Dutroux said, moving to leave. "I know a place."

Barcomb slammed Dutroux's back to the wall with one hand and shoved the barrel of his Glock to his cheek. "Where do you know?"

"A place, man! Come on!"

"You remember me," Barcomb said. "And you must remember my old partner."

"Look, motherfucker! That shit was just business! That's all! I did him quick!"

"Barcomb, we need to get-" Munday began.

"Business?" Barcomb said. "You put his head in a box and send it to Infernal Affairs. What sort of business is that?"

Dutroux cracked a smile: "Fed Ex?"

Barcomb shattered his nose with the butt of his weapon.

"Motherfucker!"

Barcomb dragged him back to his feet and got real close. "Now, you're out of ammo, you piece of shit, and you ain't got nothing else to help us through this. I could kill you right now," Barcomb said. "Say something to stop me. What place do you know?"

21

"In the hills, homes." Dutroux tried to wipe blood from his nose. Barcomb gave the back of his head a slam against the wall. "Shit, man! It's not my place, OK? I know the guy. It's like a fuckin' fortress up there, I swear to God, man."

"Who? Give me a name."

"Look, man, this fuckin' guy. You won't know who the fuck I'm-"

Barcomb slammed Dutroux's head against the wall again.

"Torrento, man! Shit! His name's Torrento!" Dutroux tried to hold his aching head and Barcomb knocked his hand away. "He's big time, man. This motherfucker, he makes my shit look like nothin'. I put your partner's head in a box? Big fuckin' deal. He'd send you the rest piece by piece and, if he fuckin' felt like it, he do the entire family like that, too. He's into some real fuckin' Columbian-style shit, homes. But it's like a motherfuckin' fortress up there. I know the guy. He's a fuckin' psycho, but - you know - he likes me. I can get you in, no problem."

"Where does this Torrento guy live?"

"I ain't stupid, man," Dutroux laughed. "I tell you that, I'm as good as dead. No fuckin' way, homes."

The stairwell door above banged open. Munday grabbed Barcomb by the shoulder. "Barcomb," she said. "We gotta get the fuck out of here right fuckin' now. Let's go."

Barcomb looked back at Dutroux: "You just made yourself useful again." Barcomb took out his cuffs and stuck them on him. "You try to run, I'll cut you in half."

Chapter 3: The Competition

They reached the ground floor quickly with Barcomb on point and Munday pulling Dutroux along at the rear. Barcomb yanked the fire exit open and looked around. The street was full of people screaming and the undead shrieking. Cars had crashed. Plane parts had fallen from the sky. People begged for death as they were being eaten alive by their friends, family and neighbors. Blood flowed in the gutter.

"The back is safer," Barcomb said. "The way we came in. We get back to the car." He looked at Munday: "Don't fire unless you really have to. Low profile. Got me?"

Munday nodded.

Dutroux looked scared. "What do you think started this shit?" he said. "You think it's some kinda punishment?"

"Call it what you want," Barcomb said. "I'm surviving this shit, wherever it came from. I got too much to live for."

Barcomb looked around, checked his mag, and then nodded.

"We go now," he said.

Moving swiftly through the yard, they weaved between the burnt out cars and abandoned shopping carts. When the ground gave way beneath Barcomb, he landed hard on his arm. He felt something wrap itself around his ankle and turned himself around to look. An almost completely rotted corpse, its flesh green and gray and almost dripping off its bones, had hold of Barcomb and was tearing at his pants. Barcomb took a moment to realize what he was looking at, to comprehend it. This corpse was years-dead, and still it hungered.

Barcomb kicked at it and a cloud of dried blood and gray brain slime erupted as the top half of its head broke completely free and it slumped still half-buried in the ground. Barcomb looked up at Dutroux, who hadn't moved a muscle to help. "What the fuck is this? This is a graveyard?" Barcomb said.

Dutroux shrugged. "When we don't feel like going to the bay, we just bury my competition in here."

Six different sets of skeletal hands clawed up through the dirt and grasped at the night air. "Business must be booming," Barcomb said.

Out of the corner of his eye, Barcomb saw much more freshly dead person. He raised his gun and looked down its sights. It was a woman, all fucked up. Blood coated her short shorts and her day-glow tube top. She was a prostitute. Her head was dangling almost free from her neck. She'd been done with an axe, from the look of it. The head dangled almost completely sideways, only hanging on by a few shreds of flesh. The body ambled slowly forwards towards Barcomb. Barcomb turned his head to get a better look at the face and immediately recognized her.

It was Rhona, his informant.

"What the shit..." he said, trailing off, lowering his gun. He took a moment, and then anger rose up inside him and he looked at Dutroux. He drew his gun on him.

"Wait!" Dutroux screamed. "I didn't do that shit!"

Barcomb pinned Dutroux to the floor and pushed his gun barrel into his mouth. Dutroux tried to speak through it, but it was too muffled. He just got spit all over the gun.

"You fuckin' scumbag, I should've shot you the second I laid eyes on you."

Dutroux kept trying to speak.

Barcomb took his gun out of Dutroux's mouth, turned and shot Rhona in the face. She fell in a heap.

"That wasn't me, man!" Dutroux shouted. "That was my competitor, homes! I swear to God! Those motherfuckers, they came in here and they fucked everything up. They couldn't have a better time to kill all my boys, because now the motherfuckers are crazy cannibal undead shit."

"What happened?" Barcomb growled, his hand on Dutroux's throat.

"It was just a buy, man. That's all. Wasn't even a big one. These fuckin' guys show up I ain't seen before, talking all kinds of bullshit. They got all their shit up in my place, then they pulled and started massacring motherfuckers. Some senseless shit, man. And one of those motherfuckers had an axe, man, I'm telling you."

"Let's get going," Munday said.

Barcomb looked Dutroux square in the eye and said, "When we came here, our plan was to kill you. That was it."

"Man, motherfuckin' police don't kill people like me. Do you know how many connected motherfuckers I know? Your life would be over, man. Don't even think it. Don't even dream it."

"Dutroux," Barcomb said, "that's still the plan. And I'm gonna be the one who does it."

They got up and moved quickly across the street and between boarded up houses, through a rusted playground, arriving at the car. Barcomb got in the driver's seat and Munday put Dutroux in the back with her.

"If we're gonna get to Torrento," Barcomb said, starting up the car, "we're gonna need help."

"The cops are all busy, man, and my Elizabeth crew just got massacred," Dutroux said.

"Don't worry," Barcomb said. "I know just the guy."

*

25

"The airport's on fire," Munday said, looking out the window as Barcomb gunned the car between abandoned vehicles and over dead bodies on the elevated freeway. Huge shafts of black smoke rose into the sky, almost glowing in the moonlight. The air traffic control tower was burning, exploding in small flashes.

Barcomb tried to put it out of his mind. He didn't need any more distractions. He had a place to go and all he had the room to think about was how to get there. Any other thoughts only multiplied his chances of getting dead. He'd been in firefights before and distractions were the number one killer. A guy distracted is a guy with one foot in the grave. But, as Barcomb was telling himself this, he looked up into the dark sky and saw a set of six lights, two red and four white. The lights circled the freeway and got larger and with them came a sound like thunder. The lights stopped circling as they got behind them by a half mile back, and then they just got slowly larger again as the noise intensified.

A plane was attempting a crash landing on the freeway.

"What the fuck!" Dutroux screamed. "They can't land that shit on here!"

"Everyone shut the fuck up and hold on," Barcomb said.

The plane, a commercial 747 likely full of hundreds of people, wavered from side to side and gained on the car. The freeway was littered with abandoned vehicles and bodies and the road was slick with blood. Barcomb slammed through an open car door as he checked his mirror. He looked over his shoulder to make sure he wasn't imagining things.

He wasn't.

The plane was bearing down on them fast and there was no off-ramp for a mile.

"Just stop, Barcomb!" Munday shouted. "It'll overshoot us!"

"That thing's gonna take out the whole goddamn freeway and it'll take hours to get around another way," Barcomb said. "Just hang fuckin' tight!"

Barcomb's foot hit the floor and the speedometer trembled, struggling to stay at a top speed of 120mph. Every jerk of the steering wheel threatened to send the car tumbling onto its side. He side-swiped car after car as he bolted through the traffic jam. Almost no-one was left in the cars. When he saw one of the undead hunched over a bloodied baby-carrier in the middle of the road, Barcomb didn't stop. He swerved and demolished the dead maniac completely, its insides splashing up the windscreen.

Barcomb hit the wipers.

The roar of the closing 747 was near-deafening. Its front spotlights now dazzled Barcomb in the rear view mirror. It was gaining fast.

"What the fuck is that?" Dutroux shouted, pointing ahead.

"Shit," Barcomb said.

A gas tanker was ablaze on its side in the middle of their side of the freeway. Around it were the burning wreckages of a ten-car pile-up. Charred bodies squirmed inside the ruins, howling in pain. A car carrier truck had jack-knifed and its load of a half-dozen car wrecks had been thrown to the road.

Barcomb spotted its top ramp. It was down. The trailer was aimed at the other side of the road. Might just get us over the divide, Barcomb thought. But it might not either. Scraping against abandoned cars and chewing up rotten limbs in its wheels had slowed the car to 60mph. Barcomb sped up.

"What the fuck you doing, man?" Dutroux shouted over the roar of the 747's engines. It was nearly on top of them. It started to descend.

The Chevy hit the trailer's ramp at 90mph and with a kick was launched into the air, clearing the truck's cab and the concrete divide, heading for the other side of the freeway.

"Shit!" Dutroux screamed.

The car was level with the pilot's window of the 747 as the car leapt and the plane smashed down onto the freeway, cars exploding around its landing gear and tearing it off almost immediately.

Barcomb head-butted the dash when the car finally hit the ground, buckling the wheels and sending it into a spin. He saw the nose of the enormous plane rushing towards them and instinctively hurled himself against the steering wheel to spin the car in the other direction. The sudden change sent the car into a barrel roll towards the edge of the freeway and soon it was airborne again and hurtling over the side of the freeway to the street below.

The plane crushed the traffic beneath it, smashing through the gas tanker with a huge explosion that started in the cockpit before smaller explosions were triggered in the wings. An instant chain reaction led the small explosions in the wings to become one immense firestorm which engulfed the entire plane as the freeway bent and cracked beneath it.

The Chevy hit the street below on its side with a loud crash.

Silence followed the booming sound of the freeway collapsing under the weight of the exploding 747. The car lay dead on Deer Park Road, surrounded by well-kept three-story apartments and trees lining the street.

Minutes passed with no movement. And then the car started to rock back and forth on its side as Dutroux panicked.

Munday's arm was snapped in three places and hung like a tail on a piñata, limp and lifeless, seemingly just stuck on and bearing no relation to the structure of the rest of her body. Shards of bones stuck out from her flesh, but she was unconscious. Munday's peace didn't last for long, however. When Dutroux shook her she awoke with an ear-shattering scream.

"Shut the fuck up!" Dutroux shouted. "You're gonna bring those fuckin' maniacs around."

Barcomb opened the rear door from outside and looked in.

Dutroux jumped. "Shit, man," he said. "I didn't even see you get out."

"Let's get going," Barcomb said. He wiped blood from his forehead and flicked it off his hand, looking around and squinting into the distance. He pulled Munday out of the car and took away her handgun, giving it to Dutroux. He kicked the trunk to loosen it up and yanked it open. Grabbing a matte black shotgun and a box of shells, he said, "It's not far. We can make it if we hustle."

In the distance was the roar of burning jet fuel and the creeping sound of manic screams getting closer. The undead were coming, like moths to a flame.

*

Barcomb led. Dutroux helped Munday along behind. Munday bit her hand as she tried not to scream. Her blond hair was black at the ends, dipped in her own blood. Tears streamed down her face. They passed a pet store with a broken window and Barcomb could only hear the squeals and barks of the scared animals inside. A small dog lay in the window on its

29

side, a terrier with its stomach clawed out and its leg bitten almost completely off. Barcomb could see the shadow of one of the undead rushing around the store killing and tearing the flesh from everything living. The dying dog made him stop in his tracks.

"We can't stop here, man," Dutroux said.

The dog with its insides on the outside looked up at Barcomb, its eyes completely glazed over in unprecedented agony the likes of which the dog could never have imagined. Barcomb drew his weapon and fired at close range. The dog's head exploded and its misery disappeared along with its face.

"What the fuck?" Dutroux said.

The undead attacker inside popped up into the light shining in from the street and spotted Barcomb. It hissed. Barcomb scowled and fired again, hitting it dead between the eyes.

"Fuck you do that for, man?" Dutroux said. "What the fuck are we supposed to do now if those fuckers hear that and come for us?"

"We fuckin' walk faster, Einstein," Barcomb said.

They reached Evelyn Road minutes later without spotting more of the undead, only dozens of the regular dead, their heads caved in or shot or cut off by the people of Elizabeth who had by now either fled the city or joined the undead.

"We're here," Barcomb said. "He's at the end of this street."

Evelyn Road sloped down a hill and they had a view of the neighborhood and the city beyond. Barcomb could see Newark. The lights of the Prudential Center still shined. Smoke rose from the area around it. The stadium held nearly 20, 000 people and tonight was the Devils and the Rangers,

"The Battle of the Hudson River", and every one of those seats would have been filled.

"Holy. Fucking. Shit." Dutroux let go of Munday and she dropped in pain, squawking as her broken arm hit the ground. Dutroux looked at Barcomb. "What the fuck do we do with this shit?"

Barcomb saw that the Prudential Center must be empty now. Looking around the neighborhood, it was like looking at a swarm of ants escaping a burning nest. Thousands of people were running and screaming and tearing at each other. Gunfire popped all around. People were still fighting. And Barcomb noticed something else.

"Wait," he said. "These fuckers are eating each other as well."

The undead attacked one another as much as they attacked the living.

"They're turning on each other," Barcomb said.

"They're fuckin' nuts," Dutroux said.

"They're dead," Barcomb said, "but they're stupid. They can't tell the difference between dead meat and live meat. They just want to destroy."

"Who the fuck cares?"

"It gives us a window."

"You wanna go in there? Are you fuckin' high, man?"

"We're going in," Barcomb said. "My buddy is down there."

"Your buddy is fuckin' dead, homes."

"Not this guy. He's got more guns than the entire police force."

Barcomb looked back at Munday.

31

"If we can get to him," Barcomb said, "He can help get us out of the city. He can get us to Torrento's place."

"We ain't going in there on foot," Dutroux said.

Barcomb spotted a bus. Blood dripped from the door. The driver inside was feasting on his passengers. "We'll take the bus as far as we can, smash through as many of the fuckers as we can, then we're up. Follow my lead."

Munday was sobbing to herself on the floor, holding her arm.

"Stand up, Munday," Barcomb said. "Stand the fuck up or lie the fuck down and die. Your decision."

She looked up at him with her blue eyes bloodshot, her face splattered with her own blood, the only clean spots where her tears had washed it away. She looked down.

"Fine," Barcomb said. He walked away from her, towards the bus. Dutroux walked after him.

"Wait," Munday said quietly, and then louder, "Wait for me."

Barcomb knocked on the bus window near where the driver was wolfing down the flesh of his passengers with his head down, buried in a pregnant woman's stomach and devouring the contents greedily. Barcomb knocked again, hard. The driver lifted his dead. Barcomb shielded his eyes with one hand and fired his shotgun with the other. The driver's skull flew through the opposite window of the bus in a million shards and his brains evaporated into a fine mist.

Evelyn Road was a war zone. Barcomb, Dutroux and Munday climbed into the bus and readied themselves to drive into it.

"If your buddy's dead already," Dutroux said, "this is suicide, homes."

"If my buddy's dead," Barcomb said, "we ain't getting out of this city alive anyway. Buckle up."

Chapter 4: Sledgehammer

The red-brick, four-story townhouse on Evelyn Road was swamped by the undead. A woman on the top floor clung to the window frame and her young son while screaming prayers at the top of her voice as she stood on the outside window ledge. When a fire-ravaged face appeared at the window, she screamed in horror and jumped backwards. It was the last thing she ever did and that face, its lips burnt back to reveal broken shards for teeth, was the last image her son ever saw. They painted the sidewalk red with the blood splatter.

Barcomb didn't take his eyes off that house as he slammed his foot down on the gas and sent the bus hurtling through hordes of the undead. The thuds and the bumps of them going under the wheels was constant. Heads cracked open against the windshield and coated the glass with thick blood. Barcomb put on the wipers and kept going. He kept telling himself these were no longer real people. A glance out the window at them tearing each other limb from limb confirmed it; these were something else entirely.

The bus skidded to a stop outside the townhouse.

"He's in the basement," Barcomb said, looking out the window.

Two corpses came crashing through a window on the second floor, hitting the ground head first with a pop, as their brains smothered the sidewalk. Gunfire sounded from the second floor in short bursts. It sounded like a machine gun.

"OK," Barcomb said with a smile as he stepped off the bus. "He's probably on the second floor."

A shirtless man appeared in the broken window on the second floor and looked down. He had close-cut blonde hair, his face was dripping wet with blood and his huge, muscular frame filled the window. He held a sledgehammer in one hand and a spinal cord in the other, the still living head dangling from the bottom moving its mouth in surprised O

34

shapes. Both dripped with blood. "Barcomb?" he shouted. When Barcomb looked up, the man grinned. "Son of a bitch! Get your ass up here, bro!" He threw down the surprised-looking severed head and laughed: "We're all having a great fuckin' time!"

The head landed at Barcomb's feet and popped as it hit the ground.

The man turned in the window and Barcomb saw him swing his sledgehammer with both hands, taking someone's head clean off with a fountain of blood hitting the ceiling.

Dutroux shuffled up beside Barcomb, looking concerned. "That crazy Arnold Schwarzenegger-looking motherfucker is your boy?"

Barcomb laughed. "That, my friend, is Eddie 'The Sledgehammer' Haws."

Dutroux nodded. "Well, alright then," he said. "Let's get him on our fuckin' side!"

Inside the building, it was the first time Barcomb had heard the undead screaming more than the living since the nightmare began. Thunder sounded upstairs as Haws's sledgehammer smashed the undead against and through the walls.

Barcomb, Dutroux and Munday reached the second floor as Hawes walked out into the stairwell. He grinned and shook his head. "Don't trouble yourself with this floor," he said, pointing at the blood-soaked sledgehammer, "ain't none of them getting past this shit."

Barcomb and Haws shook hands as Haws shot Dutroux and Munday a look.

"Who's this?" Haws said.

"Just a little help I picked up on the way," Barcomb said. "Munday's with me. Dutroux's the piece of shit we were taking down when the whole world went crazy. He even looks at you funny, you go right ahead and break his face."

Haws squared up to Dutroux and stared him down. Dutroux held his ground for about a third of a second before taking a step back.

"Nah," Haws said. "This motherfucker ain't gonna try any shit with me."

"He knows a place," Barcomb says. "He's got a guy in the hills, just outside the city. House like a fuckin' fortress. His name's Torrento."

"Torrento?" Haws said.

"He's big time," Dutroux said. "He's knows me. He'll let us in."

Haws rested his sledgehammer on his shoulder, above the skull tattoos. "He fuckin' better," Haws said, "because I'm going in anyway whether he likes it or not. No reason to stick around this fuckin' place. TV was saying this is going on all over the world."

"We'll get somewhere safe and then see what's what," Barcomb said.

"These fuckin' zombies are everywhere," Haws said.

"Zombies?" Munday said.

"Shit," Barcomb said. "That's fuckin' it. I didn't wanna say it, but you're right, man."

"Zombies, lady," Haws said, smiling at Munday. "These dead cocksuckers are walking around and eating every goddamn thing. They're zombies. What's the matter? You never seen a fuckin' movie before?"

"We need guns," Barcomb said.

Haws nodded: "You've come to the right place."

*

Haws's basement studio looked like a war bunker. A single bed and a kitchen area were the only indicators that someone was living here, and the bed was bending under the weight of bags of ammunition and the stove was simply another shelf for gun parts. This was the room of a man who was training for war. A heavy-duty punch bag hung from the ceiling and each wall was covered with a variety of handguns, machine guns and rifles. Barcomb even spotted a bazooka.

"This is home," Haws said, his hands spread out. "If you're hungry, tough shit. All I got is guns and ammo. There's probably a bagful of grenades lying around here somewhere too, so watch where you sit unless you want your asshole decorating my ceiling."

Haws grabbed an AR-15 rifle off a wall laced with assault rifles and loaded it. He handed it with a bagful of full magazines to Barcomb and said, "Merry Christmas, brother."

Barcomb looked the gun over and smiled.

"If you've got all these guns," Munday said, "what the hell are you doing running around with a sledgehammer?"

"I like my sledgehammer," Haws said. "Don't tell Pete Rose how to hit a baseball. Don't tell Tommy Morrison how to throw a punch. I got this. I'm good at violence. It's what I do, lady."

"Guns are easier," Munday said.

"But where's the fun in that?" Haws said with a grin, toweling the blood off the end of his sledgehammer.

"We're gonna need a lot of ammo," Barcomb said, throwing the AR-15 over his shoulder. "If this guy Torrento won't let us into his little fortress, we're gonna have to take it."

"Man, I know this motherfucker," Dutroux said, "he's gonna let us-"

"No offense, Dutroux," Barcomb said, "but any friend of yours ain't exactly a friend of mine. If he's half as much of a fuckin' degenerate piece of shit as you are, I'm gonna want to go in there armed to the fucking teeth."

"What we gonna do about this bitch?" Dutroux said, pointing at Munday curled up in pain on the floor.

Haws rushed over and grabbed Dutroux by the throat and lifted him into the air. Dutroux gasped and kicked and turned red. "Bitch?" Haws said. "Who you calling a bitch, bitch? You talk to your mother that way, little man?"

Haws dropped Dutroux on his ass.

"My mother was a whore," Dutroux said, under his breath.

"You good, Munday?" Barcomb asked.

She looked up with tear-streaked eyes.

"I do not give a single, solitary fuck how you feel, to be honest," Barcomb said. "I am not your fuckin' friend and I am not your fuckin' babysitter. To survive this, you gotta take care of your own fuckin' self. If you fall behind, that's where you stay. And there'll be no-one around to bury your sorry ass."

Haws tossed her a shotgun.

"Get your shit together, Munday," Barcomb said.

Haws pulled out a map of Elizabeth and a red marker. "You," Haws said to Dutroux. "Hey, fat Shaft. Come here. Where the fuck is Torrento's place?"

"No fuckin' way, man. I ain't telling you shit."

Haws held out the pen and frowned.

"Look, I'll take you there."

"If you die along the way, we're left with our dicks hanging in the wind," Haws said. "So, how about this? Either you take this pen and draw a big fuckin' X on the map where this bastard lives, or I take this pen, stab you in the fuckin' eye, and draw an X on the map myself with your blood while you think about what a fuckin' dumbass you are."

Dutroux took the pen.

"We're gonna need wheels," Barcomb said.

"We're gonna serious wheels to get out of this shit storm," Munday said.

Barcomb said, "Buddy around here somewhere?"

"Who's Buddy?" Munday said.

"Buddy can lend a hand," Haws said with a smile.

*

The townhouse backed onto a large warehouse and yard for Hambone Trucking. All the trucks were long gone and all that lay around the yard was scrap, old tires and truck parts. And something under a giant green sheet.

"I can't believe you got Buddy going again," Barcomb said.

Haws nodded and petted what was under the sheet. "Took some doing, and half my wage down at the dockyard, but I got this bad boy going good as new. He's ready for anything."

Haws pulled the sheet away to reveal Buddy, an enormous military Humvee painted entirely black. It gleamed in the moonlight. Far off human screams and zombie shrieks echoed around the yard.

This'll do the job, Barcomb thought, smiling to himself.

"Wish I'd got around to putting that turret on," Haws said.

Dutroux shared a look of disbelief with Munday.

39

"But we can always bust out the mini-gun, I suppose," Haws said.

"We need to hit somewhere for supplies," Barcomb said. "I'm sure everyone else has had the same idea, so we better move fast."

"What about the Twin City supermarket?" Munday said. "It's away from the stadium, a little on the outskirts. Nice part of town. Should be quiet. Probably has a few other things we could use."

"That'll do," Barcomb said.

Haws fired up the Humvee and they all felt the roar as it kicked in. It rattled them to their very bones. Barcomb was stood on the back with a mini-gun resting on a tripod, the ammo piled up on the floor beside his feet and his AR-15 on his back. Munday and Dutroux were sat inside, Dutroux with an MK-12 sniper rifle dangling out of the window and Munday with a two-tone EAA Witness Elite Match, the kind of pistol which can take a head clean apart and with which it's pretty hard to miss at close range.

Haws had a Desert Eagle on his belt and his sledgehammer rested on the front passenger seat. Dutroux and Munday were made to sit in the back.

Haws gunned it out of the yard and towards the outskirts.

West 73rd was bedlam.

Carson Avenue was a war zone.

Samasko Street was Hell on Earth.

Haws couldn't stop smiling.

Buddy ran like a dream and barely registered a bump when Haws pounded through acres of zombies. Some were freshly dead, soaked in blood with insides hanging from their torsos like garish fashion accessories; some had been dead

40

some time, their skin discolored, their bodies bloated or emptied after autopsies and their movements slow and clumsy due to being half or completely blind after their eyeballs had rotted out of their head. The freshly dead, they were fast, agile, angry. They locked onto the sound of the Humvee and sprinted towards it in a frenzy. They threw themselves at it in a fury and almost all were destroyed under the wheels, their brains crushed beyond recognition. The older dead, they stumbled through the streets in a daze, confused, sad, their rotting carcasses barely holding them upright. Some crawled, dragging their rancid, lifeless legs around.

Haws smashed through them all, as happy as he'd been in years.

"Don't get me wrong now," Haws shouted back in response to the disapproving look from Munday. "This is a terrible tragedy. A horrible waste of human life. I feel bad for the people who died. But these things I'm hitting right now?"

A fat old lady hit the front of the Humvee and exploded in a shower of blood and stomach fluids.

"These things," Haws continued, "they ain't the same people any more, you know? Shit. They're just like cattle now. Ain't no sin in killing cattle. Whatever made these people human, it's all gone. Now they're just zombies."

"What if they're not zombies?" Munday said.

Dutroux and Haws both looked at her with their very best "What the fuck are you talking about?" expressions. Munday turned red.

"OK," she said, looking out of the window. "They're zombies."

Dutroux leaned forward excitedly, pointing out the window at a lone zombie isolated from the crowd with a huge gold chain around its neck. "Holy fuckin' shit, Haws!" he said. "You get that motherfucker I'm gonna buy you a fuckin' gold watch. That shit's the mayor!"

Haws scowled at Dutroux. "Sit your fat ass back down now. Don't you be comin' up here in the front, you son of a bitch. Tell me what to do one more time and you're fuckin' walkin'."

Dutroux sat down and sulked.

Haws couldn't help but smile a little as he made a small adjustment in his steering as Buddy barreled down the road at 70 miles per hour.

Bam!

The mayor was cracked in half by Buddy's front grill, his legs going under the Humvee and his upper half going over it, wailing. Dutroux nearly wet himself laughing.

Munday sighed.

*

Barcomb ducked as the top half of the mayor flew past his head. He frowned and shook his head. He was itching to use the mini-gun, but there wasn't much in the way of targets. Haws was doing too good a job of crushing them all under Buddy's wheels.

Elizabeth was in utter chaos. People fought in shop fronts, looters and zombies getting blown away by shop keepers and Elizabeth P.D. Elizabeth was a shit hole, Barcomb had no doubt, but it had never been through a major crisis. He wasn't sure she would survive this. With the destruction on this scale, he wasn't sure anyone could.

Barcomb suddenly found himself wondering about the future. It wasn't something he was prone to giving much thought to. Barcomb was always a head-down kinda guy. Whatever went wrong, that's just the way it was. If things were going great, well, that was OK too. Despite his

42

penchant for violence and quick temper, he was an understated guy. He wasn't one for drama. He wasn't easily troubled by things. Things had happened in his life that would send most people upstate to the men in white coats, but Barcomb took everything in his stride. His muscular physique gave off the impression of a solid core, an almost unmovable force, and his personality was much the same.

One thing, however, really had moved Barcomb. And however much he tried to shake it, the moment kept coming back to haunt him.

Ash.

His dead partner's widow.

Barcomb had picked her up in his own car on his day off and taken her down to the station. The lieutenant had called on him first to tell him what had been delivered in the mail. The lieutenant showed up at Barcomb's door with a face like Barcomb had never seen. Officers had died in the line of duty before, but this was something else. Barcomb knew straight away that Jimmy was dead. Barcomb took a minute. When the lieutenant told him what had happened, Barcomb took a knee. His strength left him all at once. His partner was dead and his head was in a box in the station. Jimmy's head was evidence now, nothing more. Immediately, he thought of Ash. They had been married less than a year. They were still in the honeymoon period. Everything was great and her and Jimmy were the best thing that had happened to one another. Barcomb had always had a thing for Ash. She worked at a diner near to the station. That's where he saw her. That's where Jimmy saw her. Jimmy just made a move first. These things happen, Barcomb always thought.

Jimmy's head lay in a box in the morgue.

These things, Barcomb remembered thinking, they're not supposed to happen.

Barcomb took Ash up to the lieutenant's office. He had to tell her Jimmy was dead. She didn't take it well. He couldn't bring himself to tell her how he'd died. When she heard that, she headed for the nearest bridge and Barcomb had to talk her down.

When she had to formally identify Jimmy's head, Barcomb and her hit the bars afterwards and they didn't see daylight for a week.

I have to find her, Barcomb thought.

Barcomb turned to face forward, the wind making his face sting in the cold. A severed arm flew towards his head and he turned sideways just in time to let it fly by. He pulled up his radio.

"You trying to get me killed back hear, Haws?"

"Sorry, brother," the reply came. "Having too much fun is all."

"I need to ask a favor," Barcomb said.

"Detour?" Haws asked.

"Detour," Barcomb replied.

"Who is she?"

"Her name's Ash. She lives in Holbrook Heights."

"Holbrook Heights? That's right next to that massive cemetery, isn't it?"

"I know I'm asking a lot."

"Fuck that," Haws said. "Let's go to the fuckin' cemetery! It'll be a great fuckin' time!"

The radio clicked off and Barcomb heard an enthusiastic "Yee-hah!" from inside. Barcomb smiled.

As hard-assed, head-cracking psychopaths go, Barcomb thought, Haws is a good fuckin' dude.

44

The Humvee pulled a U-turn in the road and Barcomb nearly lost his mini-gun. Within moments, they were headed for Holbrook Heights.

If she's alive, Barcomb thought, she'll be needing help. If she's dead, I'll kill every son of a bitch in sight.

Chapter 5: Caged

Driving through the dimly lit neighborhoods of Elizabeth on the back of a Humvee with the sound of screams and explosions in the distance, Barcomb felt like he was at war. He wasn't sure what it made him, but he liked it.

A zombie on a rooftop screamed as the Humvee passed its building. It threw its arms in the air and ran after them, right off the edge of the roof. It crashed through the sunroof of a parked sedan and exploded inside, tinting the windows very red.

Barcomb laughed.

They might be scary, he thought, but these things are dumber than a bag of bricks.

Inside the Humvee, Munday stared out the window at the passing destruction. Her eyes were glazed over. She was in shock. Her arm had stopped bleeding, but her clothes were soaked through in blood. Dutroux eyed up Munday's pistol. He glanced in the rear view mirror and nearly shit in his pants when he saw Haws looking back at him through it.

"Everything alright back there, Munday?" Haws said.

Munday came out of her daze. "What?"

"Stay frosty, Munday," Haws said. "Don't you start sleeping on the fuckin' job."

"I'm fine," she said.

Dutroux sat forward to talk to Haws. "Look, man," he said. "Where'd you get all this gear from, yo?"

"I know people," Haws said.

"You got better shit than me and I thought I knew *everybody*!"

"Maybe you're just not a people person."

Barcomb's voice came on the radio. "Slow it down," he said. "We're coming up on a supermarket. This might be a chance to get some supplies along the way."

Haws saw it down the street. It was a Frankenfood's.

"Goddamn it, Barcomb," he said. "I ain't eating that Frankenfood's dollar store shit. I don't care if it is the end of the fuckin' world."

"Pull in to the parking lot. We'll take a look around. Beggars can't be choosers."

Haws hit the steering wheel hard.

"You don't like Frankenfood's?" Dutroux asked, confused.

"My mom used to shop here. I fuckin' hate this place. It's a fuckin' bullshit, cheap-ass store full of cheap-ass shit."

Haws pulled into the parking lot.

"Well, it's not got any better, homes," Dutroux said.

In front of the store, a police officer was pushing a shopping cart full of cans with one hand and firing his handgun wildly into a crowd full of looters with another. A stampede was underway to get out of there. People were pressed against walls until their ribs snapped in their chests and trampled until their skulls collapsed in their heads.

Haws stopped the Humvee and Barcomb leaped down from the back. Haws wound his window down to talk to Barcomb.

"What you think?" Haws said.

"Something in there is scaring them out," Barcomb said. "Must be zombies."

Gunshots sounded from inside the store. People ran screaming past the Humvee with arms full of cheap-ass food.

"We wait until it passes, guard the Humvee, and then we see what all the noise is about. Maybe we can get some good shit out of there, enough to last us until the army arrive."

"You think they're bringing the army to fuckin' Elizabeth?" Dutroux shouted from the back. "To *Elizabeth*? Man, you fuckin' high. Don't nobody give no shit about Elizabeth. Every motherfucker in a uniform on this side of the country is either headed for DC or New York. That's just the way that shit goes."

"You might be right," Barcomb said. "But we need food. We're not surviving jack shit unless we help ourselves. Whatever comes after, we'll deal with that when we come to it. For now, we gotta prepare."

Haws looked at the crowd of hysterical looters. "Looks like everyone else had the same idea."

The crowd started to thin.

Barcomb said, "Dutroux, come with me and Haws. Munday?"

Munday wasn't paying attention.

"Munday!"

She snapped to and looked at him.

"Fuckin' wake up. You watch Buddy. Anyone tries to get in or even looks like they want to start some shit, you blow their fuckin' knees off. You got me, Munday?"

She nodded and climbed into the front seat as Haws got out. She chambered a bullet in her pistol.

Haws went around to the other side and grabbed his sledgehammer. "Let's see what's shakin'," he said.

Barcomb, Haws and Dutroux walked towards the Frankenfood's Supermarket.

48

"Don't I get a gun, guys?" Dutroux said.

Haws handed him a combat knife.

"Fuck am I supposed to do with this?"

"Make me a fuckin' sandwich," Haws said.

Barcomb laughed.

"Just stay out of our way," Haws said. "And be a good boy and jump in front of me if one of those fuckin' zombies comes flapping its arms at me out of nowhere, OK?"

Dutroux spat on the ground. "This is some bullshit."

*

Inside Frankenfood's, under the buzzing yellow lights, the floor was slick with dark blood. Staff and looters lay down with gaping wounds on their throats, their faces, their bodies, and with faraway looks in their eyes. One or two moved and groaned. Dutroux took his knife and pressed the point into the skull of a woman in a green apron. She began a "Please", but the blade hit her brain before she could finish it.

"What the fuck is that?" Barcomb shouted. He punched Dutroux and he hit the floor. "What the fuck are you doing?"

"That bitch was gonna turn, man!" Dutroux said.

"She was still breathing!"

"She was done, homes! She was all fucked up!"

Barcomb put a boot on Dutroux's wrist so he let go of the knife and he pointed the barrel of his AR-15 at his head. "We don't kill people," Barcomb said. "Zombies is different."

"Bitch was gonna be a zombie, just like your boy in Hell House!"

49

Haws kept an eye on the store. The lights were off in the rear. The entrance to the warehouse was pitch black. He had the sledgehammer in his hand and a tactical shotgun on his back.

"Then you fuckin' let her turn," Barcomb said. "Do what you like when they've turned, but you ain't no fuckin' doctor and you don't know that help isn't on the way. You leave them turn."

"Fuck you know about dying?"

"I worked these fuckin' streets for over ten years. You don't get ten years in Elizabeth P.D. without taking a few lives. I took a bullet or two, as well. I've had that wait, lying around in some shitty alleyway with a fuckin' hole in my lung, waiting to see if someone would come before I'd drown in my own blood. I know guys like you. You send teenagers out to do the dying and the killing for you."

"Fuck you, man."

"Get the fuck up," Barcomb said. "Pick up your knife."

Dutroux did as he was told.

"If you stab anything that isn't dead, I'm gonna take that knife off you and shove it up your fuckin' nose until it comes out the back of your fat fuckin' head."

"This ain't the way to do it. You want to survive, homes?"

"Do you?" Barcomb squared up to him. "The law is still the law, and I'm still police. Kill if you gotta, but if you kill when you don't gotta, I'm fuckin' coming for you."

Barcomb turned and saw Haws stuffed five packets of beef jerky in his pants. Haws stopped.

"What?" Haws said, laughing. "I'm stealing beef jerky. Not the same thing, bro."

A banging noise sounded from the warehouse, metal on metal.

"We better check out the back before we load up," Barcomb said.

When they hit the Health and Beauty section on the way to the warehouse, the lights had gone out. They slowed and took deliberate steps, listening for zombies or looters. Barcomb stepped over a small body and tried not to take it in. The kid had been trampled to death. His head had been split open like a smashed watermelon. The blood looked almost purple.

"Jesus," Haws said.

The came to the warehouse entrance. Haws took the right, Barcomb took cover behind a forklift, and Dutroux hung back. The sound of metal banging continued. They heard a cry of frustration. Barcomb motioned with his hand for Haws to go in three, two, and they round the corner with their weapons drawn.

"Don't shoot! Please!"

Barcomb and Haws stopped.

A skinny kid with a hipster beard and thick glasses was trapped in a small cage, the place where the generators were kept. He wore the Frankenfood's uniform and held a large wrench in his hand which, at this moment, he was waving over his head in a panic.

"I'm not one of them!" he screeched. "I'm OK!"

Barcomb scoped out the room quickly before lowering his weapon. The loading bay door was open. He nodded to Haws and Haws went over and shut it with one pull.

"Dutroux!" Barcomb shouted. "Get your fat ass in here! Ain't nobody here to hurt you, you pathetic sack of shit!"

Dutroux walked in, trying to look confident and failing.

"Listen, please," the kid in the cage said. "Can you let me out?"

The cage was surrounded by the bodies of five or six other Frankenfood's employees. Barcomb looked at it and immediately knew what was going on.

"Can you? I'll die in here," the kid said.

Barcomb checked the lock. It was padlocked from the inside.

"I don't have a key," the kid said.

"What's your name?" Barcomb said.

"Duke." He nodded furiously. "McBride. Duke McBride. That's me. Can you let me out?"

"Duke," Barcomb said, "why are all your co-workers piled up dead around you while you sit safely in a cage which has been locked from the inside?"

"Oh, shit," Haws said sarcastically. "We got ourselves a real hero, here."

"Look, I didn't have time to think!" Duke said, bordering on tears. "I know these people. I like them." He looked down at the corpses and pointed to a girl. "Well, OK, not all of them. But I liked that one."

"Don't think you'll be getting that hand job you were after now," Barcomb said.

Haws stopped. "Hey," he said. "You think these things fuck each other?"

Barcomb turned and raised an eyebrow.

52

"For real," he said. "I seen 'em eat every motherfuckin' thing that moves. I seen them claw each other to shreds. These things don't give a fuck."

"Why would they fuck?" Barcomb said.

"News said they eat because of instinct," Haws said. "Well, people fuck because of instinct as well. It's one of the major food groups as far as instinct goes. So why wouldn't they fuck?"

Barcomb didn't know what to say.

"I mean, shit would be nasty," Haws said. "You'd have things fallin' off, things gettin' stuck, and all kinds of smells like you ain't never dreamed of, but-"

"That actually makes a lot of sense," Duke said.

"I'd fuck one, she was hot enough," Dutroux said, nodding with a faraway look in his eyes.

"OK," Barcomb said. "Shut up. Everyone, shut up."

Barcomb shot the lock on the cage. Duke cowered and squeaked, not expecting it.

When Duke got to his feet, he moved sheepishly out of the cage, stepping over the bodies of the colleagues he had so bravely left outside to die.

Barcomb looked at Haws and said, "I think I should hit him."

"I think you should too," Haws said.

"No, wai-" Duke said, before Barcomb's fist knocked him on his ass.

Barcomb turned back towards the entrance. He grabbed a nearby shopping cart and rolled it over to Haws. He grabbed another one for himself.

"Let's get some shit and get the fuck out of here before more of those motherfuckers show up."

Duke nursed his jaw on the floor.

Barcomb headed for the canned food aisle. Haws headed for the liquor.

"Haws, dude," Barcomb said, "we need food."

"I don't give a fuck if it is the end of the world," Haws said. "I'm gonna have myself a nice big crate of beers and watch it go down from this big fancy castle on the hill you guys are always talking about."

Barcomb laughed, shook his head and made for the Spaghetti-Os.

He rounded the corner of the aisle and a box of Fruit Loops exploded next to his ear. Barcomb instinctively ducked and turned out of the way, placing his back against the end of the aisle and shouting.

"Elizabeth P.D.!" he shouted. "Put your weapon down, quickly and quietly!"

"Fuck you, pig!" came the response, with three more shots fired from two different positions.

At least two shooters, Barcomb thought. Could sure use some back up.

The shelving units were seven feet tall and heavy as shit with all those boxes and cans loaded onto them. Barcomb couldn't believe it when he saw the one next to him swaying and then toppling over with a huge crashing sound and a couple of screams from underneath. Barcomb rounded it and saw Haws standing on top of the overturned shelves. He swung his sledgehammer down hard between the shelving with a sickening crack and screams like Barcomb had never heard.

Haws walked over and said, "Relax, bro. I'm playing by the rules. I only killed their legs."

"Please, man!" came a cry from under the shelves. "I got kids!"

"Shoulda thought of that before you fucked with my friend, you cocksucker," Haws said.

They loaded their carts - about an even split between beer, spirits and food - and headed for the exit. Dutroux tailed behind and Duke followed sheepishly.

Walking into the parking lot, it was like a small gladiator arena, full of dismembered limbs and dead people in various states of being eaten by rabid zombies. A few people put up a fight, but were quickly swamped and devoured by packs of the undead. There was no running from them either. Those who tried to run were quickly caught. Zombies run on instinct, Barcomb thought. So they don't save energy. They go all out, full speed, all the time. There's no running from the freshly dead. You have to fight.

And fight he did.

Barcomb's AR-15 fired like a dream, almost purring in his hands after being fired. It tore through legs, disabling the zombies, and it shredded skulls like they were made out of papier-mâché. Haws started with the sledgehammer and popped head after head, some even flying clean off the shoulders. Dutroux and Duke hung back. Duke was in awe.

"Where the fuck did you meet these guys?" Duke said. "They're like fuckin' superheroes."

"Shut the fuck up, kid," Dutroux said. "Keep an eye out."

Barcomb and Haws slaughtered their way through the bustling parking lot. Barcomb hopped on top of the hood of a sedan and climbed onto the roof. He took a knee to stabilize himself and kept on thinning the crowds. He had enough ammo to invade a small country, but he still took his time and lined up his shots. Barcomb didn't know how long he'd have to make them last, so he fought smart.

He spotted the Humvee across the parking lot. Munday was hanging out of the driver's side door and clearing the area around her. When Barcomb got her attention, he waved her over. She gave a thumbs up and got behind the wheel. The engine roared into life, enough to attract the attention of a dozen zombies right before she plowed through them and crushed them under Buddy's enormous tires. She pulled up next to the entrance and Duke and Dutroux started loading the supplies while Barcomb and Haws kept the horde at bay.

Haws was on his twentieth kill and starting to sweat.

"We nearly done here, Barcomb?" he shouted. "These motherfuckers keep on comin'!"

Barcomb saw another couple dozen zombies running at full speed across the street, attracted by the noise of the gunfire and the Humvee. "OK!" Barcomb shouted. "Let's fall back to the Humvee and get the fuck out of Dodge!"

Barcomb turned back to the Humvee, which was parked fifty yards back.

"Motherfucker!" he shouted.

Munday, Dutroux and Duke were surrounded by men with shotguns and rifles. They were shouting at Munday to put down her gun. She did as she was told. The one who seemed to be the leader wore a baseball hat and a police uniform. He had a large mustache and a big smile on his face while his men tied up Munday, Dutroux and Duke and threw them in the Humvee. He touched the Humvee with appreciation. The rest of his men were dressed like civilians.

Before Barcomb could say anything, Haws fired across the parking lot. The attackers ducked down and took cover, returning fire. The leader shouted and pointed to the

Humvee. There were six men in all and three bundled onto the back of the vehicle while the others piled in. The leader got in the passenger seat and one of his men drove. The Humvee lurched ahead and smashed through a ring fence and onto the road.

"Sons of bitches!" Haws shouted. "They're not getting away with that shit!"

"Quick!" Barcomb said. "Get in!"

Barcomb jumped inside the car he was stood on top of, a blue-gray Toyota Corolla, and pulled out the wiring. Within sixty seconds, the car rumbled to life. Barcomb hit the gas.

Who the fuck was that cop? Barcomb thought.

Chapter 6: In Pursuit

"You're losing them! They went up Thirty Third!" Haws was anxious as Hell. He'd put a lot of time and a lot of love into that Humvee and he'd be damned if some fuckin' punks took it from him now. Barcomb was gonna make sure that didn't happen.

The Toyota was a weak-ass car for weak-ass drivers, Barcomb thought, and there was no way it could keep up with Buddy in a straight race. But this wasn't a straight race. Debris, human and otherwise, littered the roads. Barcomb's only hope was that something slowed them down.

"Who the fuck were those guys?" Haws shouted.

"I don't know, but we'll catch 'em," Barcomb said. "They'll soon see they just fucked with the wrong people."

"Take a right!" Haws shouted.

Barcomb yanked the wheel to the right and they sped down an alley between two strip joints. The car sent trash cans flying and a few living people jumped out of the way. The dead, too ravenous to think of such things, ended up doing somersaults over the hood of the car.

A zombified stripper hit the hood and her head pierced the windshield, getting stuck. She gargled and hissed and tried to bite her way through as Barcomb gunned it onto the next street. Haws punched it in the face, but it wouldn't come out.

"Come on!" Haws shouted.

Haws lost patience and grabbed the zombie stripper by the head and started pushing down against the broken glass. Blood filled the car.

"Aw, man!" Barcomb shouted. "What the fuck!"

"It's a shame man!" Haws shouted. "She's got a great ass!"

Haws groaned and pushed so hard down on the zombie stripper's head that the glass of the windshield went right through her neck and out the other side. Her body tumbled to the road and Haws was left holding her head in his hands. Her head still hissed and snapped at him. Haws held her up by the hair.

"She reminds me of my ex," he said. "I might keep her."

Barcomb laughed as he wound down his window. "You sentimental bastard," he said. He grabbed the head and tossed it out. It bounced off the hood of another car and landed in the gutter.

"You're no fun," Haws said.

"There they are!" Barcomb said, pointing ahead to the Humvee.

Buddy was swerving in the road to avoid the hordes of zombies and the police officers engaged in a running battle with them. They were entering Elizabeth's modest financial district. This miniature Wall Street had three banks. Two of them, from the looks of it, were in the middle being looted by crowds of people. The other was full of zombies which were snacking on those who tried to loot that place.

World's gone to Hell, Barcomb thought, and the first thing these fuckers can think of is to go robbing banks. Maybe we deserve to die out.

Barcomb got the car within a block of the Humvee, but it was hard keeping up. Every zombie he hit massively slowed the car down, and he didn't want stray arms and legs getting tangled up in the wheels.

"This car's a piece of shit," Barcomb said. "We're never gonna get anywhere with this bullshit."

Barcomb looked ahead.

59

"I got an idea," he said. "Take the wheel. I'm gonna slow us down for a second. Soon as I get out, you floor it and keep on at them. Don't fuckin' lose them."

"What the fuck are you up to?" Haws asked.

"Trust me, bro."

Barcomb let up on the accelerator and Haws grabbed the wheel. Barcomb checked the bullets in his Glock. Enough, he thought. He threw the AR-15 strap over his shoulder. The car slowed right down. The Humvee was getting farther away.

"See you in five!" Barcomb said, and he jumped from the car, tumbling in the road.

The car almost swerved out of control as Haws took the reins, but he muscled it back into a straight line and got into the driver's seat. His foot hit the floor.

Barcomb grabbed his arm. That hurt like a motherfucker, he thought. Then he saw what he was after. There was a dead motorcyclist on the road with his helmet on. Barcomb ran over to him and looked around.

"Where the fuck's the bike?" he said to himself.

A zombie came up behind him and Barcomb opened up his skull with a pistol-whipping.

"There!" he said, spotting a white superbike with red flames painted on the side, a Honda Fireblade. "That'll do the trick."

The keys were still in the ignition and the motor was still purring away. It had been a few years since Barcomb had ridden a motorcycle, but he felt right at home as soon as he pulled it up off the ground and got on. He could see Haws in the distance taking a right turn. Barcomb revved the bike and took off like a tornado, hitting a hundred miles per hour in a matter of seconds. The force of the bike going past knocked over a zombie as he raced to catch up with Haws and the Humvee. He didn't know what he was going to do when he caught up with them, but he knew he needed to get to them. Too much was at stake now. That Humvee and that food and those people, he thought, they might be the difference between two more weeks of living and two more years.

The Fireblade moved like a dream, floating through the streets and responding to his slightest touch instantly, roaring to life when he needed it and gliding around the corners. He felt the wind in his face and the AR-15 rattled around on his back as he leaned into the corners. He couldn't help grinning. He'd missed this.

He gained on Haws in the shitty Toyota in no time. He sped up beside Haws's window, gave him a signal to keep going.

"Cover me!" Barcomb shouted, knowing it was probably lost under the sound of the Fireblade's engine.

He hit the throttle and the bike raced ahead, picking up speed as it navigated through the carnage in the street.

Barcomb weaved between upturned cars and jack-knifed trucks and dodged zombies of all shapes and sizes that sprinted towards the oncoming sound of his engine. Haws took a few out behind him as he tried to keep up. Barcomb saw them being flipped into the air, spinning as they went and leaving an arching spray of blood in their wake, as they collided with the Toyota.

The Humvee was up ahead. Barcomb couldn't see inside the tinted windows. The wind in his face was making things difficult. The Humvee hit a zombie and it exploded into six or seven parts on impact. Barcomb thought fast and swerved aside as the upper torso of the zombie flew towards him. He saw it bounce under the wheels of the Toyota which, by now, was losing considerable ground.

When Barcomb's Fireblade was within a few yards of the Humvee, it suddenly swerved to cut Barcomb off. They'd spotted him. A rear window opened and a Latino kid of about twenty years old hung out and started popping at the bike with his pistol. The bullets hit the tarmac. The kid was a shitty shot.

Barcomb wasn't.

He drew his Glock and fired three rounds. One hit the kid in the neck and slumped over the window, dangling out with his necked opened up and pouring blood all over the road. Barcomb holstered the Glock and quickly swerved to avoid the blood. If I come off this fuckin' thing at this speed and hit my head without a helmet, he was thinking, I'm as good as dead.

The Latino kid bounced past in the road and hit an upturned car, his back snapping in two with a crunch even Barcomb could hear over the sound of the bike. The bastards must've just tossed him out the window, he thought.

Barcomb zipped the bike around the side of the Humvee and could see Munday and Dutroux thrashing around with someone in the back, throwing punches and elbows. The three on the open back of the vehicle finally got wise to what was going on and scrambled for their guns. Barcomb drew his Glock and got a shoulder-shot on one and flustered another one to the point where he panicked, stumbled backwards and fell over the side, hitting the road head-first with his neck spinning right around killing him before he could even realize he wasn't on the Humvee any more.

They were coming up on the Strip in Elizabeth, Barcomb realized. This meant trouble. Elizabeth was by no means a tourist-friendly spot. It appeared on no lists of "Places to visit on the East Coast". In fact, the only lists Elizabeth routinely appeared on was "Most dangerous cities in the USA". This, however, didn't deter visitors. It merely changed the type of visitors the city drew in. Elizabeth drew in the criminal element and the sleaze, the low-stakes poker crowd and the retirees who didn't know any better. These people crowd out the Strip every night until sun-up, looking for marks, johns, lays or coffee houses with nice waitresses. The Strip was up and on the right.

Don't turn right, Barcomb said to himself. Don't you fuckin' dare turn right.

Barcomb swooped around a fist fight in the middle of the street and righted himself. He looked up just as the Humvee turned right onto the Strip.

Shit, Barcomb thought.

*

The Strip was lit with a hundred neon lights for topless bars, massage parlors, xxx-rated movie theatres and second-rate casinos. The moon was hidden by the neon haze that blocked out the night sky. The sound of the Strip was usually one of shouted offers, mumbled replies, screamed demands and hurled abuse. Tonight, it was all shrieks and screams. Barcomb slowed the Fireblade and glided around onto the Strip. There must have been a thousand people on the street, two-dozen police cars and a score of ambulances. A couple of bloodied fire trucks were parked outside the Lucky Larry Casino. A group of firefighters lay face down with holes in their heads as huge flames licked out of the windows of the hotel above the casino. The road was littered with corpses and smashed and burnt-out cars, debris of all kinds. But Barcomb didn't give a shit about what wasn't moving. He was too busy looking at all of the people and the zombies running and fighting and bleeding and killing. He could barely tell who was alive and who wasn't. Some areas were just fine red mist flying in the air with arms and legs thrashing beneath. Others were clearer, with groups of zombies literally tearing people into pieces, yanking at heads and tearing at necks and chewing at arms.

Human beings still tried to scream even after their heads had been separated from their bodies. This is a fact that Barcomb could have lived happily without knowing. Now, he had seen the evidence first-hand. He could sense the nightmares in the future, if he lived long enough to have them.

Haws was approaching behind, the Toyota slowed through the barrage of bodies that had bounced underneath it and become tangled in the inner workings. Barcomb didn't have time to wait. It was dangerous to go ahead, but he couldn't lose them. He couldn't lose the supplies. The Humvee charged forward through the crowds of people, crushing them under its huge wheels and smashing aside any wreckage on its way through. Barcomb hit the throttle and followed in its wake.

The wheels of the Fireblade struggled to gain traction on the road slick with blood. Barcomb had to take it down to forty miles per hour and go easy on the turns, which was tricky with so many bodies and so much scrap metal lying around and being bounced back by the Humvee twenty yards ahead. Zombie hands grasped for Barcomb as he rode by, coming close to unseating him when they touched the bike.

Barcomb's radio buzzed with static. He forgot it was clipped to his belt. A voice sounded from it, Texan and brash. The other handset was in the Humvee.

"Give it up, partner," the man said. "You ain't getting anywhere in this shit storm. Do yourself a favor: tuck your tail between your legs and run off home now, ya hear? And don't you worry about your friends. We'll take real good care of them. Especially the woman. Gonna treat her like a real princess, aren't we fellas?"

Laughter sounded in the background. Munday started to scream, but the radio cut out.

Calls himself a cop and he pulls shit like this, Barcomb thought. I'm gonna fuck him up.

Barcomb gunned it, maxing the bike out. The Fireblade got right up to the rear of the Humvee. Barcomb drew his Glock to shoot a tire. Fuck it, he thought. Better fuck the whole thing up and get our shit than have this prick keep it!

The Humvee suddenly jerked under the weight of a huge crash as it slammed between two wrecked cars. The wrecks span violently in the road, their rear ends closing fast on Barcomb as the Humvee pushed through. Barcomb cleared the first car and the second slammed into the back wheel of the bike.

Barcomb was airborne.

*

Something ached. Something else stung. There was one part which was hurting like a bastard. He thought he heard something crunching when he tried to move. It wasn't pleasant.

That's good, Barcomb thought. I suppose that means I'm alive

He opened his eyes.

"Fuck me," he said.

The world was upside down. Upside down signs flashed red at him, asking him if he wanted a massage. Upside down cars burned in the street. Upside down zombies looked in his direction and screeched. His upside down AR-15 had been thrown from his back and lay a few yards away. Barcomb righted himself. He was lying on the now broken windscreen of a VW beetle. He stood up. The woman sat behind the driver's seat might have been angry with him if she still had a face with which she could express emotion. Her skin had been torn from her face and the muscles and fat

65

underneath had been chewed to the bone. She lay there dead, looking awfully sorry for herself. Barcomb cracked his knuckles and rotated his shoulders. His left shoulder gave him a poke, shooting with pain. He looked and saw a shard of glass sticking out. He yanked it free and tossed it to the ground.

"Goddamn," he said.

Even more zombies were looking in his direction.

Barcomb pulled his Glock and checked his mag. Seven rounds left.

The AR-15 was close, but not close enough. A horde of zombies we slowly coming to the realization that Barcomb was alive and alive meant tasty. The Fireblade lay amid the horde. Barcomb lifted his Glock and fired at the gas tank. He missed with two shots, tried again and only hit the seat. A zombie stepped in the way. Barcomb grimaced. He lined up his sights properly, head shot the zombie and then pinged the gas tank exactly right, sending it up in a huge explosion which threw the zombie horde back and set them on fire.

Barcomb jumped down from the car and grabbed the AR-15. He looked up and the burning zombies were running at him, noisier and madder than ever before. They were too close to take one at a time, so he sprayed their legs and cut them all down in their tracks.

The smell of their burning flesh and hair was unbearable.

Barcomb spun around to survey his surroundings. He'd been thrown quite a way. He was right in the middle of the Strip. Zombie blackjack dealers and undead hookers were everywhere. Barcomb was, in a word, fucked. He ran to the fire trucks outside the burning casino and climbed up the back. The explosion had brought a huge crowd of zombies, all of them starving, hungering for warm flesh. Barcomb had seen them attack one another - it seemed any flesh was good when times were hard - but they clearly preferred their meat warm and wriggling in agony.

Over the rabid screams of the undead, Barcomb heard a familiar voice. He didn't like what it said.

"Fire in the hole!" Haws shouted.

Barcomb looked just in time to see him pull the pin on two grenades and toss them into the crowd surrounding the fire truck. Barcomb ran towards the other end of the truck and jumped onto the ground. He got to his feet and the explosion threw him back down. Limbs and bones, the flesh disintegrated off it, erupted in the middle of the street, like a morbid geyser. Barcomb moaned in pain and slowly pushed himself up off the ground. He looked at Haws, stood a few feet away next to the shitty Toyota.

"Was that really necessary?" Barcomb said.

A warm, red shower started as the blood from the victims started to fall from the sky. Barcomb accepted it, standing there frowning as he was soaked red.

Haws nearly smiled.

"Where the fuck is my Humvee, Barcomb?"

"They got away," Barcomb said.

Haws shook his head and cursed under his breath. "Well, we'll get it back. We'll get it."

"Damn straight," Barcomb said. "Does it have GPS?"

Haws nodded.

"We're gonna need some help getting it back," Barcomb said, "assuming they stay in the city."

"I need a computer to track it," Haws said.

"I know someone who has one."

"Ash?"

Barcomb nodded. "She's pretty handy with a gun as well."

"Maybe she can lend a hand?"

Barcomb nodded.

"OK," Haws said. "Lead the way."

Barcomb opened the driver's door on the Toyota.

"Fuck that Toyota shit, though," Haws said. "Let's get us a real fuckin' car."

"What you got in mind?"

Haws nodded to a sky blue Dodge Challenger with twin white stripes. It was parked on the side of the road, untouched but for a few scratches. "I'm driving," Haws said. "Where's this chick live?"

"Next to the cemetery," Barcomb said. "There might be a lot of these zombie bastards around there."

Haws grinned. "Let me just grab my sledgehammer."

Chapter 7: Cemetery Dance

The moon was yellow in the sky, but it was at least visible now away from the neon glow of the Strip. One or two stars - they might have been planets, Barcomb wasn't sure - shone through the light orange haze created by the streetlights. Looking at the stars, it made Barcomb wonder about how all this shit started and it was all going down in the rest of the country. Was it radiation from a crashed satellite? Maybe it was a science experiment gone wrong, some kind of disease warfare? Could be it was just Hell had come to Earth and these were the last days. Barcomb decided it didn't matter. All that mattered was that he survived it with enough - enough people, enough supplies, and enough guns - that he could have something approaching a life afterwards.

He turned on the radio.

Static with small snippets of speech. He fiddled with the dial.

"What was that?" Haws said. "You had something there."

Barcomb turned the dial a tiny amount at a time, the static breaking way for a voice underneath the noise here and there.

"Unprecedented violence-" it said.

Barcomb twisted it.

"global-"

Barcomb frowned. He tried again.

"After the death of the US President-"

"What the fuck?" Haws said.

"-and the resignation of British Prime Minister David Cameron after he accepted responsibility for the crisis, the world looks for leadership. Reports of wide-scale destruction and death tolls in the hundreds of thousands are reported all across the country, with little sign of it slowing down. Elsewhere, the effects have been no less devastating as France is left without a functioning government and London has been evacuated. The US government has called on island nations to accept American refugees, but Australia and Ireland have refused, despite having successfully contained the crisis in their nations."

"That's it then," Barcomb said.

Haws nodded. "The world is fucked," he said.

"We're on our own."

Haws said, "How the fuck is it even the Aussies can get their shit together, but we're flapping around like dumbasses and can't even protect our own president?"

Haws took the car around the burning wreckage of a news channel helicopter. Barcomb tried not to look at the thrashing arms and legs within the fire. Haws leaned over and rummaged in the glove box.

"Let's see what we have," he said.

He pulled out a stack of CDs and then opened his window. Leaning on the steering wheel with his elbows, he started tossing the CDs out the car one at a time.

"Shit. Shit. Lame. Shit. Embarrassing. Shit. Shit."

Barcomb looked out his window just in time to see a man plummet to his death from an apartment window. Shit is just too much for some people, he thought. Have a safe trip.

Haws laughed. Barcomb looked over. He held up a CD and grinned: "Motorhead," he said.

The zombies could hear them coming from over a block away, but Haws drove so fast there wasn't a thing they could do to get in their way. They entered the nicer part of town, but the scenery didn't improve. Death and chaos at every turn. There were more dead bodies than alive people, and more hunger-crazed zombies than either. A couple of the zombies tore at each other, which interested Barcomb because they could just keep going until both were literally just a torso with a pair of arms attached. The zombies didn't care after a while if they were attacking a human or a zombie; they'd rather go after a human for the warm meat, but instinct was instinct and cold leftovers would do just as well. Zombie gladiator matches. There's something in that, Barcomb thought. Zombie MMA. ZFC.

The arrived outside Valhalla Cemetery and pulled over.

"This girl," Haws said, "I didn't want to say shit before, but she's living in a fuckin' cemetery?"

"Nah," Barcomb said. "She's not a fuckin' vampire. She lives on the other side, but it's a thirty minute drive to get there or a five minute walk through here. Road system in this city, man. It's fucked. I'd say go round, but we don't know what the fuck is waiting around there. Least this way, we know these motherfuckers are all old dead. There shouldn't be much fight in them."

"You think?"

"Yeah. I'd be surprised if half of them even got out their fuckin' coffins. You see Kill Bill? Took that woman fuckin' hours to get out of her coffin and she was a fuckin' kung-fu master. Some dead as shit old corpse isn't getting out of that shit without some real fuckin' effort."

Haws grabbed his sledgehammer and jumped out the car. "Well, I hope some of them did. I'm feeling pretty pumped!"

Barcomb got out his side and they both approached the entrance. It was locked. Haws smashed the large padlock with his sledgehammer and kicked the iron gates open.

"Wakey-wakey," Haws said.

71

Valhalla Cemetery was a wooded cemetery with birch and oak trees masking its enormous size and the number of graves inside. Its gates and fences were wrought iron, painted black, and the caretaker's office was built from stone and had Victorian-style, long windows with wiring. The first grave Barcomb saw as he walked in featured a weather-beaten, stone gargoyle on top, about to take off and snarling viciously. As they walked down the path, keeping an ear out for suspicious sounds and an eye out for moving ground, Barcomb noticed that the older a grave was, generally, the scarier its gravestone was in design. He figured attitudes towards death had become much more friendly in the last fifty years or so, with terrifying gargoyles replaced with statues of kindly angels and photographs printed into the stone of smiling portraits of the dead.

These zombies will fix all this chicken shit "Death is just another destination" type motherfuckers, and no mistake, Barcomb thought. Nothing brings the terror of death home like having a re-animated corpse tearing the skin off your face and eating it for breakfast.

Haws was quiet.

"You OK there, buddy?" Barcomb said.

"I remember this place," Haws said. "I been here before. When I was a little kid."

"You sure? You always lived the other side of town."

Haws nodded. He gripped his sledgehammer tight.

"I got lost in here once," Haws said. "Spent the night hiding in the doorway of a crypt type thing in the pouring rain."

"All night?" Barcomb said.

Haws nodded. "No-one came looking for me."

"Fuck."

"Just being here, it's making me real fuckin' angry."

Barcomb nodded ahead. "How about you take it out on something?"

Farther up the path, two zombies were pathetically fighting each other, clawing and biting as they both lay on the floor, their legs too rotten to let them stand up. They clawed slowly and pitifully, doing no damage. Their graves had been dug open from the inside. They hadn't gotten very far away from them. Haws walked over. He lifted his sledgehammer up, then brought it back down slowly. He put it down on the floor. Then he stamped on one of the zombies, putting his boot heel right through its half-rotten skull. He stomped the other one too, its brains splattering up his pant leg. Then he jumped up and down on them like a little kid jumping in a pool.

Barcomb watched, his eyebrows raised.

Haws stopped and looked up.

"Um," Barcomb said. "We feeling better?"

Haws grinned. "Much," he said. "Though I think I got some blood in my shoe."

Haws took off one boot and a sock and wrung the sock out, the blood dripping on the path.

"If there's one thing I can't stand in this world," Haws said, "it's wet goddamn socks."

There was a low murmuring sound up ahead, around a small hill and past some trees. The two of them moved quietly and quickly. Barcomb was ready to fire. As they neared, the low murmur became a loud collective moaning sound, earthy and guttural, sounds from things which should no longer be making sounds, their voice boxes having rotted into disuse long ago.

73

In the middle of the cemetery was a lake the size of two basketball courts with a small island in the center with a single grave in the middle; it had a statue of a dog on top of a small pillar. Barcomb didn't give enough of a shit why to ask. The whole lake was surrounded by rotten zombies lying on the ground, their eyes turned to jelly and their muscles chewed to nothing by the worms long ago; they were like a huge carpet of blind rotten meat with teeth. There was too many to walk through.

"Man," Barcomb said. "We'll be here all night if we want to kill enough of these to make a path."

"How about a swim?" Haws said, pointing to the lake.

Barcomb spotted a row boat and laughed: "How about a romantic boat ride, bro?"

"Buy me dinner after?"

"Not a chance."

They headed for the handful of zombies between them and the boat. Barcomb was able to hit them with the butt of his AR-15 and cave their skulls in, no problem, preserving his ammo. Haws took a couple out bare-handed, punching through their temples and coming out the other side.

"It's just like cracking eggs," Barcomb said.

*

The top edge of the boat was very close to the surface of the water as Barcomb pushed them away from the shore.

"I don't think these boats were really designed for people like us," Barcomb said.

"What do you mean?" Haws said.

"I was trying to downplay it, buddy. You're fuckin' huge. You could fill this fuckin' boat if you lied down."

Haws laughed.

"Just try not to move around too much."

The boat rocked a little with each stroke of the paddle. It was very slow going.

"We got out of a fuckin' Dodge Challenger and into this piece of shit," Haws said. "I'm get antsy. Can you hurry this shit up?"

Barcomb frowned. "Do you wanna row and I'll sit her complaining? We can switch roles, man."

Haws laughed, then sighed. "I'm bored, man. This is some slow-ass fuckin' boat ride. You row boats like old people fuck." Haws lifted up his pistol and took aim at a zombie that was trying to stand up and failing; its legs snapped under its own weight.

Haws fired and its head jerked and rolled off, bouncing on the ground.

Every single zombie surrounding the lake, roughly two hundred grey, blue and green faces in various states of decomposition, now turned and looked at Haws.

"Oh," Haws said, mildly surprised. "That's, um, not so great."

Barcomb stopped rowing. "Be quiet a minute," he whispered. "Don't move."

The zombies looked around with their melted, jelly eyeballs which saw nothing. Their ears, however, were mostly intact. The blind dead began to stir, and, one by one, they crawled into the water, like pale, starved crocodiles.

They all floated, their mangled legs trailing behind them like fish tails, and their efforts to crawl towards the boat produced a kind of eerie swimming motion that propelled them along slowly. They came into the water from all sides. Barcomb and Haws were in the boat in the middle of the

75

lake. The floated past the island. Barcomb still didn't care enough about the dog statue to read the plaque stating why it was there. He had other things on his mind.

"This is just an idea," Haws said, "but maybe you should be fuckin' rowing."

Barcomb looked around. They were surrounded. He picked up his AR-15 and said, "I've got an idea."

Haws pulled up his pistol.

"Let's fill them full of holes," Barcomb said. "They'll sink to the bottom and we can just sail right over them."

Barcomb pointed to the shore in the direction they were heading.

"This direction," he said. "You row, and I'll start sinking some battleships."

He handed Haws the paddle and got on one knee at the front of the boat with his rifle against his shoulder. There was a good twenty zombies coming from that direction and Barcomb couldn't see their faces. They didn't need to come up for air. They didn't exactly know where they were going either, he didn't think. They just heard a noise and jumped in.

Barcomb popped a few rounds into the first few zombies. They sank like bricks with a cloud of bubbles appearing after each one touched the bottom of the lake.

"It's working," Barcomb said.

By the time Haws rowed the boat to the shore, they were floating past outstretched fingers which pierced the surface of the water. They jumped and pulled the boat onto the shore in case they needed it to get back.

"That was some smart thinking," Haws said.

"And you can't row for shit either," Barcomb said. "I could've got out and swam faster."

76

"Maybe you should've," Haws laughed. "Make some new friends at the bottom of the lake. How far to this house?"

Gunshots sounded out in the night. In a dark, ten-story apartment building off the left, beyond the wrought iron fence, windows were lighting up with gun flashes.

"It's that house," Barcomb said, pointing towards the source of the gunfire. "We better get moving. It's starting to rain. Don't want wet socks!"

A feeble, skeletal hand latched onto Barcomb's ankle from a grave. The stone read: Lawrence Mendelson. Barcomb shook his foot and the hand broke off.

"Get a job, Larry," he said. "Jesus."

Chapter 8: Crazy Cat Lady

Barcomb and Haws scrambled over the fence as the rain started to drizzle down and they jumped into the shared back yard for the apartment building. Haws slipped on his ass. He looked up and saw that a half dozen little crosses made out of twigs were scattered around, stabbed into the dirt. Haws put his ear to the ground beside one of the crosses.

"Holy shit, Barcomb," he said.

"What is it?"

"I ain't shitting you now," Haws said, laughing, "but I can hear meowing!"

Barcomb chuckled.

They ran for the fire escape on the back of the building. Haws gave Barcomb a boost up and he pulled the ladder down for them to climb up. There hadn't been any more gunfire and Barcomb was concerned. He ran ahead, taking two steps at a time. Ash lived on the top floor. Why the fuck did she have to live on the top floor? Barcomb thought, as his legs started to ache. Haws was a dozen steps behind and he looked like he regretted carrying that heavy sledgehammer around with him.

Barcomb got to the top and stopped. He hadn't thought this through very well. He didn't know what to say. He hadn't spoken to her about anything other than her dead husband, Jimmy, his former partner, since Dutroux put Jimmy's head a box and presumably threw the rest away in the Bay. He didn't look in the window in case she saw him. He needed to think of something to say first. Something clever or witty or romantic. Maybe not romantic, he thought. That's coming on a bit strong. But Barcomb did have feelings for her. Always had.

Haws was clanking and clumping up the metal staircase to the top, so he had no time to prepare a grand speech. Fuck it, he thought. I'll see how it goes.

Barcomb stepped in front of the window and looked inside.

Ash was in her early twenties and tanned with raven hair. She stood at five foot six. Right now, she was stood only in her underwear, facing the television with her back to the window with a large meat cleaver in her hand. Her ass was also facing the window. Barcomb couldn't help but admire. Her ass was in very small white panties, lit only by the moonlight and the highlighted by the blue glow of the TV in the background. Barcomb had a difficult time focusing on the task at hand.

Haws got to the top. "Hey, is this-" he began.

Barcomb shushed him.

Haws looked in the window too. He struggled not to swear when he saw her. He nodded at Barcomb in approval.

Ash wander over to the coffee table, which was hidden from view behind the sofa. They could see the side of her now. Her figure was incredible. Barcomb had about two seconds to admire her before she did something which surprised him. She started hacking at something on the table. She brought the meat cleaver down again and again, splattering blood all over her body. She wiped some from her eye with the back of her hand and carried on.

Barcomb and Haws exchanged worried looks.

A hand came up from the table. A human hand. Ash pushed it away and continued hacking with the meat cleaver. The sound was sickening: crunch, crunch, crack, splash. After a few more hits, Ash bent over the table and put her foot on it. She pulled with all her might and with another crunch she

79

stepped backwards. She lifted an old woman's head up in her hands.

Actually, Barcomb saw it was a zombie's head.

Its mouth wriggled and writhed in pain and its eyes rolled all around in its head. Ash held it up to her own face using both her hands and looked at it closely. Blood spurted from the neck stump down her body, but she ignored it.

"Die," she said, looking it in the eyes.

It made screaming faces, but no sound came out. It showed no signs of slowing down or dying again. Ash held it closer.

"Die," she said.

Its blood ran down her breasts and down her stomach and legs and pooled on the carpet around her bare feet.

Haws whispered to Barcomb, "She's a fox, but she looks fuckin' crazy. You sure about her?"

Barcomb nodded.

Ash lower the zombie head and held it by the hair. She sighed and dropped her shoulders in disappointment. Suddenly, the zombie head locked its eyes on Barcomb and Haws at the window. It tried to scream and snap, but there was no sound save the clicking and clacking of its teeth as it flew into a rage. Ash moved the head back up to look at it.

"Thanks for nothing," she said to it.

Ash noticed the zombie head's eyes were fixated on something behind her. She didn't turn right away. The head was raging, snarling and biting at thin air. It had seen someone. Ash slowly leaned over and picked up her Taurus Judge, a stubby, silver handgun with a pink, rubber grip and loaded with 45 Colt cartridges. It could take a chunk out of anything or anyone. She hid the handgun by her side, out of view of the window, and casually dropped the zombie head on the coffee table. Spinning, she saw two figures at the window and fired three rounds as she ducked behind the sofa. The glass shattered and she heard a man swearing and the clatter of them diving for cover on the fire escape.

Ash waited for return fire, but it didn't come.

"Who the fuck are you?" she shouted. "Get the hell out of here! I got more ammo than you got balls and I'll shoot the little bastards off you with this fucking thing! Just you see if I don't!"

Outside, Haws wiped blood away from his eyes. She'd skimmed his head. An inch lower and his brains would be back down in the yard. Barcomb put his back to the wall and peered in the window. Another shot came and he ducked back.

"Ash!" he shouted. "Relax! It's me!"

"Me who?!" she shouted back.

"It's Barcomb! It's Darren!"

Ash went quiet for a minute.

"Who's with you?" came the eventual reply.

"It's my buddy," Barcomb said. "He's good people."

"Please stop trying to shoot my face off!" Haws shouted. "It's not good for my complexion!"

"Stay there!" Ash shouted.

"What are you doing?" Barcomb said.

"Hold your horses! I'm putting a damn shirt on!"

Haws laughed.

Ash appeared at the window with the bleeding, headless corpse of an overweight old woman over her shoulder. She stepped out onto the fire escape and looked at Barcomb and then Haws.

"Jesus," she said. "You two look like shit."

She pushed the headless corpse over the side of the fire escape and it tumbled down to the yard, hitting the ground with deep squelch sound.

"Well, don't just fucking stand there," she said, walking back inside.

Barcomb and Haws stood up and shrugged at each other. Barcomb was about to walk in when he had to dodge the zombie head that Ash had thrown through the window. It sailed down to the yard after its body. Barcomb and Haws climbed inside the apartment.

"Don't mind her," Ash said. "She was just leaving."

The apartment was nice. Barcomb had always thought so. The blood sprayed all over everything, though, somewhat ruined the cozy effect of all the exposed wooden beams and leather-bound books. There was an empty cat basket in the corner of the room.

"Where's the cat?" Barcomb asked.

"Cleo died last week," Ash said. "Buried her out back. Happens, I guess. The crazy cat lady down the hall - you just met both pieces of her - she's got a load of graves out there already, so I figured one more wouldn't hurt."

Haws winked at Barcomb. Barcomb frowned.

The door was boarded up and nailed shut. The kitchen area was stacked with supplies.

"You seem to be doing good," Barcomb said.

Ash nodded. She grabbed a cloth and wiped all the blood from her face. "I'm doing OK, considering it's the end of the world and all that jazz."

Haws flicked on the light.

"Hey," Ash said. "Don't be a dumbass."

She walked over and flipped it off.

"You want to put up a big sign to everyone saying we're home?"

"Zombies don't climb fire escapes," Haws said.

"No," Ash said, "but you did. Humans are twice as dangerous as those fucking things right now."

Ash sat down on the arm of the sofa and reloaded her Taurus Judge as she spoke.

"I went out for supplies a little while ago," she continued with that faint Southern accent of hers. "I barely made it back alive. People have turned into goddamn animals."

"We know," Barcomb said, perching on the coffee table. "We got a problem. A real big problem."

"An asshole-shaped problem," Haws said.

Barcomb and Ash looked at him, a little confused.

"Like, a man who's an asshole I mean," Haws explained. "Not an actual asshole. That would probably be pretty small, pretty solvable by ourselves. I'll shut up for a minute. You got any Spaghetti-Os?" Haws walked off to the kitchen.

"You want my help?" Ash said to Barcomb.

"I wanted to make sure you were OK," he said, "but, yeah, we need your help too. We got it good. We got a plan. We got supplies. We got a fuckin' military Humvee and a guy who knows somewhere safe in the hills."

"I might not have a military Humvee or Arnold Schwarzenegger backing me up," Ash said, "but I got supplies. I got this place locked down."

"You got this *apartment* locked down." Barcomb looked over his shoulder to the kitchen. Haws pulled open a can of Spaghetti-Os and started drinking it. "You got enough food to last you a couple weeks. What then?"

"I'm not leaving my home."

"Listen," Barcomb said. "This place, it's vulnerable. You're in a populated part of town. The zombies get wind that you're up here and swarm the place, you're gonna have nowhere to go."

"I've set up ladders on the roof. I can go across to the next building."

Barcomb was taken back a little. "Well," he said, laughing. "OK. That's real smart. Seriously. Shit. I'm impressed."

"I can take care of my own damn self," Ash said.

"But if this place is swarmed and you get up on the roof, if you even get down through the next building, where you going?"

Ash looked away.

"How many bullets you got for that thing? I mean, that's a fun little gun, but what the fuck good is that gonna do when you have to reload it after every six shots? You haven't thought this through."

"What makes your plan any better?"

"Not very much, to be honest. It's sketchy at best, and we don't have what we need. Everything we had just got taken from us. Some fuckin' dick bags stole our Humvee and three of our people, one of them the only one who can get us into this safe house in the hills. But, listen, if you come with us, you'll be set. I promise you. You'll be set until this whole thing blows over. And if it doesn't blow over, then you'll be

84

with a tough group and we'll make ourselves as safe as we can and play the hand we're dealt."

"No," Ash said. "I'm staying in my home. If the zombies come for me, they'll have a fight on their hands. If they take me," she shrugged. "I've made up my mind, Darren."

*

Haws booted up Ash's laptop and a happy little jingle played. Haws frowned at the computer instinctively. When a desktop background featuring fluffy penguins appeared, Haws was visibly doing everything he could not to just snap the damn thing over his knee.

"You're too old for this cutesy shit," Haws said through gritted teeth.

"I like penguins," Ash said. "Bite me."

"You sure this GPS shit is gonna work?" Barcomb said.

"If it's all still online and this thing can hook up to it, yeah. I'm not exactly a tech guy, but it's pretty fuckin' fool proof."

"What if they disabled it?" Ash asked.

"They ain't that smart," Barcomb said.

"Who are they?" Ash said.

Barcomb took a sip from his beer. They were all sat around the breakfast bar. "One of them was a cop," he said. "I don't think I recognized him. Must've been from the other side of the building."

"Whoever they are," Haws said, "they ain't gonna be it for long. I got a sledgehammer with their name on it."

"Seriously, though," Ash said, "what's up with this sledgehammer shit? It's a little scary."

Haws laughed and winked at her. She didn't know what to make of him.

"How you been coping, Ash?" Barcomb asked.

"With what?"

"With everything."

"I don't want to talk about Jimmy now," she said. "Thank you for thinking of me, Darren, but I'm gonna be fine here by myself. I don't need to be taken care of and I don't need to be running after a truck-full of assholes just because they stole all your shit. You can use the computer to find his Humvee, but then you gotta go."

Barcomb touched her hand and she pulled it away.

"I can't be around people," she said. "It's been less than a month since Jimmy died, and now all this. I can't take it. I just need to lock myself in a dark room and wait and see. Maybe it'll all blow over."

"We've been all over the city tonight," Barcomb said. "Ash, listen to me. This isn't gonna just blow over. We need to take action to make ourselves safe. Nobody else is coming. No-one gives a shit any more. It's every man for himself."

"The GPS is still working," Haws said. "I told you those dumb motherfuckers wouldn't realize it was tagged."

"Where is it?" Barcomb asked.

"It's just loading it up now."

Barcomb turned back to Ash. "What were you doing when we got here?" he inquired. "What were you doing with that zombie?"

"The crazy cat lady from down the hall?"

"If that's who that was, yeah."

"She got bit by one of those things. I stabbed it in the head and it seemed to die well enough from that."

"Yeah. We figured that too. Kill the brain and the rest will follow."

"The bite wasn't too bad, but it acts like some kind of poison. She was dead within an hour. Wasn't even bleeding very much."

"Zombies," Barcomb said. "All those movies had to come from something. I guess maybe one of those Hollywood fucks, somewhere down the line, must've known what he was talking about."

"Yeah. She died and turned really quick."

"But, Ash, what were you doing when we got here? What were you doing with her head?"

"It was an experiment. I didn't kill her. I took her in when I saw her being attacked when I went for supplies. I brought her in, thought she'd be OK, but she wasn't. After she turned, I disabled her legs and then just cut off her head. It took me a couple hours to work up to doing that, so don't think I've gone all psycho or anything."

"What was the experiment for?"

A tear rolled down Ash's cheek. She wiped it away.

"Nothing," she said. "I was just being a freak."

Barcomb didn't believe her. There was something to it.

"You're not gonna fuckin' believe this, bro," Haws said. He laughed.

"Where's Buddy at?"

"Home turf for you," Haws said. "They took it back to the police station, of all places."

"The police station?" Barcomb said. "What the fuck?"

"You think they've taken it over?" Haws said.

87

"Could be. The entire force would be out on the street, I reckon, and they've got a cop running their little group. If he had clearance to get in, he could get the others in, no problem." Barcomb stood up. "It's a smart move. It's one of the most secure buildings in the city. It's got a canteen, a nurse's station stacked with medical supplies, and the second biggest stock of guns around, after yours, Haws. Even got a morgue to store people in if they lose someone, or if they just want to keep their beer cold."

"You reckon we can get in there and ruin their day without being noticed?" Haws said.

"Maybe," Barcomb said. He looked at Ash.

"They're in the police station?" she asked Haws. "Definitely? They've stayed there? What makes you so sure they haven't just stopped for a minute?"

"The Humvee is in the police garage. The little blue dot on the screen hasn't moved. The stats are telling me they pretty much went straight there after they fucked us off. They're staying. They might move on in the morning, but they're there for the night at the very least."

"We got three hours until sunrise," Barcomb said. "We're gonna have to get moving."

Ash fidgeted with her fingers, staring at them, thinking.

"Ash, you got a car around here?" Barcomb said.

"My neighbor has a pick-up. It's nice. He's on vacation, too, so his apartment is empty. You can bust in and grab the keys. It's parked in the small parking lot across the street."

"What is it?" Haws asked.

"It's a black Ford, brand new."

88

Haws nodded. "I've seen the advertisements. That can explode a few zombies along the way if I get bored."

Barcomb picked up his rifle and checked the ammo in his Glock.

Haws slammed the laptop lid closed. He checked his Desert Eagle out. Full clip.

Ash stood up. She walked over to the coffee table and grabbed her Taurus Judge. She took a box of shells down from off a bookshelf and started reloading. Barcomb watched her. She looked good in a red checked shirt and torn jeans. She tied the shirt up at the stomach to stop it flapping around everywhere, exposing her mid-riff. She slipped a hair tie off her wrist and put her long black hair into a ponytail.

"I'm coming with you," Ash said. "If they're in the police station, I want in."

"Why?" Barcomb asked.

"Doesn't matter," she said. "I'm coming with you."

Barcomb walked over to her. "You ready for this? This shit is gonna get violent."

"I want it," she said. "I need to go. I've got something I have to do."

Barcomb looked at the pool of blood on the coffee table and it struck him what she'd been doing. How could he not have seen it? How could he be so blind?

"Fuck," he said.

Ash looked at him. Her eyes were full of tears.

"Look, Ash," he began, "I'm sure it's not like-"

"I did the experiment," she interrupted.

Barcomb nodded.

"I cut off that crazy cat lady's head and she still kept on ticking. She was still in pain."

"That doesn't mean-"

"It does mean that, Darren. It really does. Don't sugarcoat this shit for me."

Barcomb put a hand on her shoulder.

Ash looked up at him. Her voice wavered as she spoke: "My husband's head is in the morgue in a box," she said. "In the basement of that building, his head is probably screaming in the dark right as we speak. Jimmy's head is awake and one of them. If we don't do something, he's gonna stay that way. I can't live with that."

"You're right," Barcomb said.

"I have to do this," Ash said. "I have to finish him off. If I don't, I know he'll be like that forever. These things never just die by themselves. He's gonna suffer and suffer. Maybe there's nothing left of him in there, nothing of his personality, but I can picture him now and I want to be sure. He would do the same for me."

"It's gonna be a Hell of a fight," Barcomb said.

Ash wrapped her arms around him and hugged him tight. "Everything's a Hell of a fight now."

Barcomb petted her hair. "We'll put Jimmy out of his misery, right after we put those other motherfuckers into theirs."

"We don't got time for this namby- pamby shit," Haws said, walking past and grabbing his sledgehammer. He smiled. "Let's go fuckin' get some."

Chapter 9: The Station

Ash knocked on her neighbor's door and waited a moment, just to be on the safe side. Haws kicked in the door in one go and he, Barcomb and Ash entered, guns drawn. The layout of the apartment was mirrored to Ash's, but the decor was totally different, much more modern. There were a lot of shiny white surfaces. Barcomb hated it immediately. It looked like a hospital waiting room.

"The keys should be around here somewhere," Ash said.

"I'll see if he's got anything else we can find," Haws said, walking into the lounge.

Barcomb and Ash searched all the standard places in the hallway where people leave their keys. There was no sign.

"Sure he didn't take it with him?"

Ash nodded: "The keys are here somewhere."

Haws strolled from the lounge to the bedroom. He'd picked up a bag of potato chips along the way somewhere and was munching them down five at a time.

A noise came from the bedroom. Something like a "Huh."

Barcomb took a look.

"Oh, shit," Barcomb said.

Several chains hung from the ceiling. A rack on the wall held whips, sex toys were stacked in clear plastic boxes against the wall. Ash walked in and put her hand over her mouth.

"OK then," she said.

"So, are you big buddies with this neighbor of yours?" Haws said, raising an eyebrow.

Barcomb picked up a leather mask in the shape of a pig's face.

"This," Ash said, "this is some weird shit. You think there are zombies in the Caribbean? I'm not sure I want this fuckin' guy to come back and live next to me." She pointed at Barcomb's leather pig mask. "That's hot, though."

Barcomb put it on and looked at Haws.

Haws stared at him. "Dude," he said.

"How do I look?"

"I spent all night murdering the re-animated dead," Haws said. "I nearly got myself killed a few times out there, man. But this shit? This is the most scared I've been all night."

Barcomb laughed and took off the mask. He looked at it, said, "No shit," and threw it aside.

Ash walked out the room. "I'm gonna see if he's got any fluids around here that aren't lubricants. I need a drink."

Haws started unclipping the chains from the ceiling.

"What you doing, man?" Barcomb said.

"Chains, dude. You never know." Haws threw them over his shoulder.

"You're a thrifty motherfucker, let me tell you."

"Keys!" came the shout from the kitchen.

*

The street was clear but for a few screamers sprinting by, presumably chasing after some noise or other they heard ten minutes ago. It hadn't escaped Barcomb's notice how dumb these zombies were. One of the screamers kept falling over. It had a big bite in its leg, exposed by the short shorts the woman the zombie used to be was wearing. She must've been

92

out for a jog, Barcomb thought, because she still had big, chunky headphones around her neck.

The parking lot was almost pitch black. Ash took out her cell phone to use the screen to light their way through the cars.

"You getting any service on that?" Barcomb asked quietly.

"Nothing. Went down an hour ago and that was it. Something must've taken out the towers," Ash said.

"That or the government want us all to shut up and stop talking to each other," Haws said.

"I was wondering when you were gonna start developing some sort of weird paranoia about this whole thing," Barcomb said.

Haws laughed.

"Well, the British have claimed responsibility, those Limey fucks," Barcomb said, "so don't think about it too much. Have you heard anything much, Ash?"

She stopped beside a car, crouched down and shook her head. They all crouched and waited as a zombie with half its face burned off walked past as fast as its rotten legs would carry it, which wasn't very fast at all.

Ash whispered: "I saw some of it play out on TV. I was watching the Devils-Rangers game and they kept cutting away to talk about riots in New York City. Eventually the crowd started to thin out because people were getting home to check on their friends in the city and that kind of thing - at least that's what the announcers were saying."

"Where's this happening?" Barcomb asked.

"Everywhere," she said. "No explanation. No theories beyond extremely unlikely scientific shit and hysterical religious crap. They think it's part of some British experiment gone wrong, but their government's not talking much. Half of them are dead anyway, I think."

"No real explanation means there'll be no real cure," Barcomb said.

"Shooting them in the head is a cure," Haws said.

The burnt zombie had gone, so they got up and moved. Ash pointed to the back corner of the lot. "There," she said.

A bright red Ford F-150 sat alone. It looked clear, so Barcomb, Haws and Ash walked over, keeping an eye on the buildings towering above. Shadows shifted in the windows, frantic, running, thrashing. Every apartment building was its own separate Hell with its demons, its tortured souls, its flames. Barcomb saw a woman banging on the inside glass of a window in the distance. She was just a near-faceless shape. The faceless shape banged on the glass. Her Hell was coming to an end. Another shape came up behind her. The window turned black with sprayed blood. Barcomb looked away.

Ash clicked the keys and the car lit up. Haws opened the driver's door. "Give me the keys," Haws said.

She tossed the keys to him. Barcomb caught them midair.

"Get in the back, Haws," Barcomb said.

"Alright, bro. Do me like that," he said, grinning, "but make it right."

He took the Motorhead CD out of his back pocket and shoved it in Barcomb's hand. Ash rolled her eyes.

*

Elizabeth Police Department was housed in a turn-of-the-century townhouse, five stories tall with a clock tower, an underground garage and a front yard and an impound full of burning cars and half-eaten corpses. Barcomb slowed the

94

pick-up down to a crawl. Haws rolled down a window and stuck his head out to get a closer look.

"Stop the car," he said.

Barcomb stopped and turned off the headlights.

"Where they gonna be at?" Haws said.

"The Humvee will be in the garage, man," Barcomb said. "Where they'll be, I don't have a clue."

"What's the best way in?"

"It's a police station. There's no good way in. How much firepower we got?"

Haws held up his Desert Eagle. Ash held up her Taurus Judge. Barcomb had a Glock and an AR-15.

"I got one and a half magazines for the AR-15," Barcomb said, "and a couple for the Glock."

"I got about ten more cartridges," Ash said.

"Two clips," Haws said, "and the sledgehammer. That's it, but that's enough."

"No," Barcomb said. "It's not. They don't have many guys, but they got the station."

"Who knows how many more dudes inside," Haws said.

They sat there a moment, watching the building. The windows were all barred. The garage door was shuttered close. They could see no movement and only a few lights were visible on the top floor. A city bus had crashed through the fence around the rear lock up, where all the impounded cars were kept, but the area was swarming with the undead. It looked like people had flocked to the police station when the trouble started, but there was no help left to give. All they'd done was put themselves in one place for the zombies, a movable buffet. There was a lot of ice hockey fans too. The stadium wasn't far. The plane crash on the overpass must've brought a lot of the zombies over looking for barbecue. A handful of the zombies were fighting with one another, ripping organs out of their opponents and chomping on them. It was a mess, a mess without end because it was a fight none of them would ever win against themselves.

It was dark out, but the street lights outside the station were still going. Barcomb had parked the car in a dark spot across the road were the lights had gone out, but they couldn't get to the station without being in the light or without having to slaughter two dozen zombies.

"Top floor is probably the best bet for where they're holed up, given that's where the lights are on, but it's a big building," Barcomb said. "That might not mean shit. Getting in is the problem. We can't just ram the car in there."

"I can kill the shit out of some zombies," Haws said, "but that's gonna get noisy."

"Either of you guys got a knife?" Ash said. "I got an idea."

*

Ash jammed the knife under the zombie's chin. The point peeked out of the top of its balding head. It was a sixty-something man with a creepy moustache. Haws grabbed it under the arms and dragged it into the back of the pick-up.

"You sure about this?" Haws said.

"What's the plan here?" Barcomb said.

"OK," Ash said, shoving the knife in the zombie's stomach and slicing it open. "We can't get through the front door. We gotta go through the zombies."

"What, you trying to make us smell like zombies or some shit?" Haws said. "They do fuckin' stink. Maybe that's not a bad idea."

96

"Don't be a dumbass," Ash said. "Zombies are dead. Most of them are real fuckin' dead. They don't even have noses left on their faces, they're so rotten."

"How do they smell?" Barcomb said.

"Fuckin' terrible!" Haws laughed. He wiped some of the zombie's blood on his face.

"Children," Ash said. "I'm dealing with children."

Barcomb apologized and said, "I guess the smell thing is a dumb idea anyway. I mean, we could make ourselves smell like them or whatever, but we don't know that that's how they sense people. Most of them sense people like anyone alive. And, like you say, Ash, some of them don't even have a nose to smell with any more. Regardless," Barcomb said, "these fuckers attack each other as much as they attack the living. They just want to eat. They prefer warm meat, but if there's nothing about, they'll start on anything."

"We disguise ourselves in case any of those assholes are watching from the station," Ash said.

"And we quietly kill the ones who pay attention to use as we go," Barcomb said. "It's not great, but it's better than sitting here with our thumbs up our asses while they do God only knows what to Munday and the others."

Barcomb took a scoop of blood from the zombie's stomach and smeared it on his face. He took off his black tactical vest and stole the zombie's floral print shirt.

Ash laughed.

"Really brings out my eyes, right?" Barcomb said.

*

Barcomb, Haws and Ash didn't make the most convincing zombies - they had simply tore up their clothes and covered themselves in blood - but Barcomb hoped it would be

97

enough to fool anyone just glancing out the window. He hated that they had to be doing this. Every extra minute in the city was another minute of tempting fate. He knew the smart move was to leave, but he couldn't let Munday be taken and he genuinely thought Dutroux was telling them the truth about Torrento's little fortress in the hills. Duke was just some dumb college kid, but that didn't mean he deserved to die. And those fuckers, whoever they were - whoever that cop was - they looked like bad news. Ash had learned pretty fast in Elizabeth to read people. In the police force, you had to; you were a walking target if you didn't. You'd end up like Reyes, confused, bleeding out, and then dead.

Ash was pretending to limp across the street. Barcomb would've laughed at her hammy acting if it wasn't for the fact that they were about to walk through a horde of bloodthirsty re-animated corpses. Haws carried his sledgehammer in one hand, dangling it down low to hide it behind the crowd. In his other hand he held a shard of glass. Barcomb had a knife and his AR-15 was strapped to his back under his shirt. Ash had a knife too, and her Taurus was tucked into her jeans which were now ripped in enough places for Barcomb to get somewhat distracted as she ambled in front with her ridiculous zombie impression.

There were so many unknowns heading into this place. Barcomb was trying to manage everything in his head. He had no idea how many motherfuckers were inside. He had no idea how many guns they had. He had no idea if the zombies had got in. Shit, Barcomb thought. I don't even know if Munday, Dutroux and Duke are still alive.

But Torrento's place in the hills, it was worth the risk.

A farmhouse might be enough in the movies to keep zombies away, but, in real life, here and now, Barcomb thought, these sons of bitches were fast and tough. The fresh ones, a fresh dead skull is just as hard to get through as a living one. At least Barcomb imagined so, not being the kind of guy who's shoved a knife through a human skull before that night. We need a fuckin' fortress, he thought. And the kind of guys Dutroux knows, they're probably the exact kinds of guys rich enough and paranoid enough to live in one.

The horde of zombies in the impound didn't move in any kind of predictable way. They swarmed around like a hive of angry wasps. They were attacking each other at random, moving to strike at anything that caught their half-rotted eyes.

An overweight zombie woman in a bikini wobbled towards Barcomb. Barcomb watched her out of the corner of his eye, trying not to make any big moves to attract her attention as they neared the larger crowd. Eyes ahead, Barcomb put a hand on his Glock, just in case.

They were within ten yards of the hole in the fence. It was still blocked by a half-dozen zombies of all shapes and sizes: doctors, police, hookers, all soaked in blood, most missing hands and arms and eyeballs. Suddenly, the doctor's head popped open on one side and his brains hit the side of the crashed bus with a slap. Almost at the same time, a little after, Barcomb heard the crack of a gunshot.

Ash ducked down instinctively.

Barcomb saw right away what the problem was: someone was firing from the top floor of the station.

After Ash ducked, there came a shout. She'd given herself away to the sniper who was just thinning out the zombies.

"There's someone out here!" the shout came.

"Move!" Barcomb shouted, dragging Ash to her feet and towards the hole in the fence. Haws was way ahead of them, slamming his sledgehammer through heads and kicking some zombies to the ground. Barcomb drew his Glock and got headshots on two zombies, flooring them. He fired a shot towards the station window as he made it into the impound, but it bounced off the brick beside the window.

Ash took out a couple of zombies with headshots which shredded faces and evaporated brains at close range with her Taurus and she and Barcomb hunkered down behind a tow truck inside the compound. Haws ducked behind a wreck as a bullet ricocheted off the metal inches from his head.

"What now?" Haws shouted.

"Improvise!" Barcomb shouted back, taking out a couple more zombies that were closing in. "We gotta get in there fast before we run out of ammo!"

Barcomb peered around the side of the tow truck. He fired at the sniper in the window twice, making him take cover. Barcomb took the opportunity to pull the AR-15 from under the back of his shirt. He lined it up on the window and waited for the sniper to show his face.

The sniper popped up again and looked for them, a bolt-action rifle in his hand.

The sniper was James Dutroux.

"Motherfucker," Barcomb said.

Chapter 10: Cop Killer

Dutroux fired from the top floor of the police station. Soon, the cop who stole the Humvee, the Texan, he joined him and started firing down too.

He joined them, Barcomb thought. I should've expected that.

The cars in the impound were arranged in long rows. Barcomb turned to Ash and said, "Get down. We'll crawl through. We can't risk running out in the open. Fuckin' Dutroux is up there shooting at us, so we can't return fire either. We need him alive."

Ash's face turned pale. "Dutroux? James fuckin' Dutroux is up there?"

Barcomb grabbed her, "Listen, we don't have-"

"That piece of shit cut off my husband's head and sent it to you in a box and you're telling me not to shoot at him? That's what you're fucking telling me?!"

Ash turned and emptied her Taurus at the window. Barcomb spun her around and kissed her. She was stunned.

"Listen to me," Barcomb said. "You have to survive. I couldn't live with myself if anything happened to you. This place he knows, this fortress in the hills, this is our best shot at outlasting this bullshit. We kill him, we'll never find it. We keep him alive, he might even be able to get us inside without a fight."

Ash shook her head and wiped away her tears.

"Look," Barcomb said, "no-one wants to kill this sack of shit more than I do. No-one. And a day will come - I promise you this, Ash - when we make him bleed. I want him to die. I want him to die so slow that he gets to taste every little bit of it on his way out. But we need to be smart. Please, Ash. This is too big. This place, those supplies they have, that

Humvee: that's our ticket out of here. That's the difference between us and these dead motherfuckers wandering around. Nobody wants to die. Everyone does their best. These zombies, their best wasn't good enough."

"I want him dead," Ash said. "I'll wait, but I want it. And I want to be the one who does it."

"We need him right now. I wish we didn't, but we do. As soon as we don't, you can gut him like a fish. I started off tonight with the exact same plan. There's a cop in there, Officer Munday, and she came with me. God only knows what they're doing with her, but she came out for your husband to help me kill the motherfucker who did that to him. We're her only chance. Dutroux is our only chance."

Ash nodded and wiped her eyes.

She crawled under the tow truck.

"Head straight," Barcomb said. "You'll come to the back door of the station."

Haws jumped the gap between the tow truck and the car he hid behind. He got down on the floor and stood back up. "I ain't getting under that shit," he said. He was too big.

"Get ready to run," Barcomb said. "I'll cover you."

"What do we do when we're inside?"

"Anyone in there you don't like the look of, you smoke 'em."

Dutroux was firing at them from the top floor. He was laughing his ass off.

*

The door caved under the weight of Haws's sledgehammer and he barreled through. Barcomb and Ash followed and they found themselves in a long corridor. Before they had a chance to catch their breath, they heard the scream of zombies behind them from the impound and a storm of boots and shouted curse words running down the corridor around the corner towards them.

"Get the door!" Haws shouted.

"Up ahead!" Barcomb said. He raised his AR-15. He had to make every shot count.

Ash slammed the door shut and pulled it hard, holding onto it. "This fucking door isn't gonna hold!"

Barcomb thought fast. He grabbed a fire extinguisher off the wall.

Haws drew his Desert Eagle. "Door on the left," he said, "where's it go?"

"Stairwell!" Barcomb said. "Ash! You run for it when I say."

Barcomb tossed the fire extinguisher down the hall. It bounced down towards the corner just as three guys turned it and raised their pistols. Barcomb fired the AR-15 once and the fire extinguisher exploded.

"Now, Ash!" he shouted.

Ash let go of the door and ran for the stairwell. Barcomb and Haws were right behind her.

The door to the impound burst open and a zombie horde screeched and wailed as they barged and clawed their way past each other to get to the warm meat, the good stuff. At the end of the corridor, the three guys were floored by the explosion from the fire extinguisher and blinded by the powder. The zombies were on them before they knew what was going on. They ran right past the stairwell and piled onto the three guys.

They feasted.

It was a bloody, screaming meal. The kind the zombies loved best.

Barcomb, Haws and Ash took the stairs two at a time and headed for the top. They stopped at the double doors. Ash looked through the glass.

"Looks OK," she said.

Barcomb looked. He shook his head at Haws.

Ash looked again. Haws pulled her back as the glass exploded inwards with the crack-crack-crack of machine gun fire.

"Y'all made a pretty big mistake comin' in here!" the Texan shouted from the other side. "A fuckin' titanic mistake is what you all have made! For what? For the fuckin' drug dealer? For the college idiot? For that fuckin' pig bitch?"

Pig bitch? Barcomb thought. "Where'd you get that uniform, motherfucker?" he shouted.

"I ain't a goddamn pig," the Texan shouted. "Truth be told, I always wanted to be. And I done more than you to be a cop, let me tell you. What, you took some tests ten years ago? I had to kill a guy to get to wear this uniform."

Barcomb scowled and peered through the glass. The Texan was stood in the middle of the corridor. Barcomb fired, the Texan scrambled for cover, and Barcomb pushed through the doors and took cover behind a steel cabinet.

"Oh, yeah," the Texan said from around the corner. "I killed me a lot of cops tonight, let me tell you."

The corridor was where the top brass worked, with glass fronts and many attractive houseplants on this floor as there were damp spots and mice holes on the lower floors. Barcomb had nothing to work with here. The Texan started speaking with someone behind him around the corner as he hugged the wall. Barcomb had been up here only once. He'd been a little hard on a suspect and the police chief needed to get in a room with him to make it look like he had been slapped on the wrist. In reality, they shared a drink and talked boxing for thirty minutes. The chief even gave him tickets for that weekend's fight. Barcomb had taken the head of a suspected kiddy fiddler and given it a few solid whacks against the wall. What Barcomb remembered now, however, was how he could hear every word from the office next door and the office the door down from that.

Thin walls, Barcomb thought.

He fired through the glass at the end office and the Texan ducked. He fired three shots into the wall and the third drew blood. Barcomb had hit the Texan's second man in the head. He saw his hand hit the floor past the corner. The Texan shouted something which was lost amid the noise of him firing four rounds down the corridor in retaliation.

Barcomb heard the Texan shout off behind him, "You bring that bitch down here right now!" And as he did, Haws and Ash barged through and dived into the first office on the right. Barcomb made for an office on the left and tore the blinds down inside. He flipped a table and took cover behind it as it was pressed up to the window. He could see the Texan from inside the office.

Then he saw Officer Rachel Munday. The Texan grabbed her from another of his guys and she almost fell over as he dragged her towards her and wrapped his arm around her neck and put his gun to her bruised and bleeding head. Munday was stripped down to her underwear.

"Oh, yeah," the Texan said, laughing. "Another one of my boys got himself a uniform too! He had a real good time getting it, too!"

Munday was dazed, her left eye half shut and her right eye was swollen shut. Her good eye looked up and met Barcomb's gaze. Barcomb fought the urge to try a headshot on that Texan motherfucker right there. Barcomb heard a crash from across the way and saw Haws smash through one office into the next, using his sledgehammer to make himself

105

a connecting door. The Texan got nervous and tried to peer around the corner to see what was going on. Haws smashed through another wall.

The Texan fucked up.

He raised his gun, taking it from Munday's head and aiming towards the noise that Haws was making.

Munday bit into the Texan's arm so hard she tore out a chunk of flesh and muscle. He screamed and shoved her to the ground. He moved his gun back towards her, but Barcomb was faster. The Texan's chest exploded in three places and he hit the back wall with wide eyes, his body completely limp. Munday looked up at Barcomb with blood dripping from her mouth. Barcomb nodded.

The Texan's buddy jumped out from behind the corner. He was dressed in Munday's tactical vest.

"Motherfucker!" he shouted.

The wall exploded beside him and Haws barged through like a goddamn freight train. Before the guy could even register how fucked he was, Haws punched him so his nose went up into his brain. It was a KO he'd never wake up from.

Barcomb walked out from the office. Munday shakily stood up. She grabbed the Texan's gun, put it under his chin and fired. She turned her gun on his friend and unloaded the entire clip.

Barcomb didn't know what happened with these guys, but, seeing the look in her eyes when she turned around, he knew he could never ask.

"Where the fuck is Dutroux?" Ash asked.

Barcomb heard a door shut upstairs.

"He's on the roof," Barcomb said.

At that moment, the stairwell door smashed opened and a host of zombies broke through. They were all fresh. They were all hungry. They were all coming right for them.

Haws stepped forward and gripped his sledgehammer with both hands.

"I got this," Haws said.

"You good?" Barcomb asked.

Haws looked back and grinned. He rummaged through his pocket and pulled something out and tossed it to Barcomb. It was grenade.

"Found it in that office, bro," Haws said. "You have yourself a party up there."

Barcomb smiled.

Haws ran at the zombies even faster than they were running at him.

Barcomb and Ash helped Munday out the other stairwell door. They rested Munday on the wall.

"Ash," Barcomb said, looking up the stairs and checking it down the sight of the AR-15. "You gotta get Munday outta here."

"I'm not leaving without Dutroux," she said.

"I got him," Barcomb said. He caught Munday as she was about to fall. Barcomb took off his tactical vest and shirt and gave them to Ash, leaving himself with just a black vest and his combat pants. "Put these on her," he said.

Ash grabbed Barcomb's arm as he was about to leave.

"Listen," Barcomb said. "It's one motherfucker. I work better alone. I got this asshole. Take Munday down a flight and head right. There's an office there. Get in. Lock it. Wait for me."

"Barcomb," Ash said.

Barcomb kissed her. She didn't know what to say. She kissed him back. "Get out of here," Barcomb said. "I know what he took from you. I can't put you in harm's way again. You stay down in that office. Look out the window if you hear a noise, you might just see that son of a bitch on his way down to the sidewalk."

Ash smiled.

Barcomb checked the clip of his Glock. He had ten rounds. He took off the AR-15 and hung it around Munday.

"You giving up your baby?" Munday said, trying to laugh through a mouthful of blood.

"I'm coming back for that bad boy," Barcomb replied.

Chapter 11: Beat down

Barcomb burst through the door to the rooftop and checked his surroundings. There was a cluster of air ducts sticking up from the flat roof, a maintenance shack and a clock tower in the center. He spotted movement behind an air duct cooler and fired. Barcomb took cover behind another duct and looked around. He listened. He could smell burning flesh in the air. It was almost dawn and the city was alive with the sound of death. The zombies had been tearing through Elizabeth like a tornado, ripping apart everything and everyone in their path. Barcomb saw nothing in them. There was no humanity left. He saw them as a force of nature, like a plague or a flood, and he dealt with them in the same way. It wasn't murder if they were already dead. It wasn't self-defense even, thinking about it. It was pest control. It was flood prevention. Every zombie he killed saved a life tonight, and not just his own. Every zombie he killed was tens, maybe hundreds of victims. That's how he saw it.

That's not how he saw Dutroux.

Dutroux was straight revenge.

Dutroux had no more power. His thugs were gone; his drugs were gone; his criminal empire had been decimated. All Dutroux was now was a fat fuck with a gun and no second chances. He must've joined these motherfuckers almost right away. They didn't look like his boys. Too white. Too country. They gave him a gun and he let them have Munday. For Barcomb, that was enough. Killing Jimmy was enough. Being a drug-dealing scumbag, slinging dope in local schools and using little kids as runners, that was enough.

The man don't deserve to live, Barcomb thought. And, as shit as this world has become after this night, it'll still be a better fuckin' place if I take this son of a bitch out right now.

"You don't fuckin' quit, man!" Dutroux said. "You killed the others?"

"Don't worry," Barcomb shouted, "you'll get your turn, motherfucker!"

Dutroux fired twice. Barcomb heard the whistle of the bullets flying by over his head. Dutroux was using Munday's Glock. Barcomb bared his teeth just thinking about it. He nearly growled.

Dutroux moved for a maintenance shed at the corner of the roof. He ducked behind it as Barcomb fired. A ricochet caught Dutroux's arm and he spun to the ground. He crawled back behind the small iron shed.

"Look!" Dutroux shouted. "We can stop this shit right here, man!"

"Why would I wanna do that?" Barcomb shouted and ran for the shed. Dutroux jumped out from behind it and started firing. Barcomb felt a hot slice in his arm as he ducked for cover behind an air duct. He wasn't gonna let a small thing like a bullet through the arm stop him, and he'd be damned if a lowlife like James Dutroux was gonna be the one to stop him.

Dutroux got behind an air duct next to the clock tower. "You want to get to Torrento, you want yourself a fuckin' zombie-proof hideout," he shouted, "you go through me! He ain't gonna let you in without me!"

"Fuck your zombie castle bullshit!" Barcomb said.

Dutroux laughed. "You think that's it? You think it's just a nice fuckin' house?" he shouted. "That man, he got enough firepower to fuckin' roll through you, wherever you go, homes. You got no fuckin' chance without me. You don't need his house, man. You need him dead."

"I ain't scared of any friend of yours," Barcomb said.

Dutroux rose and fired. His Glock clicked. Out of ammo. He reached for another clip. By the time he had his hand on it, Barcomb had put a bullet through his forearm. Dutroux screamed, dropped the clip and ran for the clock tower. Barcomb followed and aimed for his legs. Running and gunning all night had taken its toll and Barcomb cursed himself for being a little off with his aim. His entire body was aching, but he pushed through. He crashed through the door and Dutroux waited on the other side.

Dutroux hit Barcomb with the butt of his Glock and drew blood. Barcomb stumbled back a moment and it was enough of a window for Dutroux to throw a punch with his other hand. Barcomb recovered fast, though - faster than Dutroux anticipated - and grabbed his wrist and twisted it around, using the force of his punch against him and slamming his head into the wall behind him. Dutroux dropped his gun and Barcomb made him all kinds of hurt. He slammed his head three times into the wall and punched him in the spine. He twisted his arm until it snapped and Dutroux dropped screaming to the floor.

Barcomb kicked him in the stomach until he coughed blood and screamed, "New Providence!"

"What the fuck did you just say?" Barcomb said.

"New Providence, man." Dutroux said. "That's where Torrento at!"

"I told you I don't give a fuck." He kicked him again.

Dutroux groaned in pain. "I told you, homes! Guns! Ammo! Enough shit to last a year! You think your boy Haws is a survival freak, man. You ain't seen shit. This motherfucker has built himself a fuckin' fortress and got enough shit in there to survive a nuclear fuckin' holocaust, man."

Barcomb thought for a second. He needed somewhere. The world had gone to shit. Torrento sounded

111

dangerous. Zombies can be out-run and out-thought; human beings were a whole other headache. If they were gonna survive this shit, zombies were only half the problem.

"I see you thinkin'," Dutroux said, laughing through broken teeth.

Barcomb shook his head. "Keep talkin'," he said.

Dutroux laughed. Barcomb picked him up and threw him against the wall. Dutroux slumped down. Barcomb stamped on his other arm and broke it.

"Garfield Drive!" Dutroux said after a minute of straight screaming.

Barcomb decided right there. He couldn't afford not to go.

We need out of Elizabeth, Barcomb thought. This is our shot.

"Barcomb!" Ash's voice sounded outside the tower.

Barcomb turned for a split second. It was enough. Dutroux kicked out at Barcomb's knee. He buckled for a moment and Dutroux was up the stairs, headed for the top.

"Motherfucker," Barcomb said.

"Barcomb!" Ash called again.

Barcomb followed Dutroux.

Barcomb's lungs burned and his knee was on fire as he pushed himself up the stairs, making footprints in Dutroux's blood. He's got nowhere to go, Barcomb thought. He's unarmed. What the fuck is he thinking? Barcomb got to the top and Dutroux was looking out over the city. The top of the tower was framework with no walls, a clock hanging from the frame. The sun was coming up slowly. The sky was as red as the streets below. Dutroux knew he was beaten. Barcomb could see it. One arm was broke, one was shot, and the guy was beat all to Hell.

"You're one stupid motherfucker," Barcomb yelled.

"Man," Dutroux said with a chuckle, not even turning around, "the world got overrun with fuckin' zombies and I still get killed by some white fuckin' cop. Fuckin' zombies, homes." He shook his head.

"You're going out either way, man. You were on your way out the moment you set foot in my city. You put my partner's head a box? Well, there we are."

"There it is, man."

Dutroux turned around. He sniffed. He was crying. Barcomb laughed.

"Yeah, man," Dutroux said. "Big, bad drug kingpin badass goes out cryin' like a bitch."

"Funny stuff," Barcomb said.

"You know, I never had a chance, homes. You know where I come from? You know how I come up, what I went through?"

"I don't give a fuck," Barcomb said.

"Ain't nobody ever given shit to me. Everything I ever got, I had to take that shit for myself. Someone else had to lose out? Some fuckin' pieces of shit had to fuck up they live on my shit because they weak and they can't say no to a fuckin' needle? Not my problem. Some fuckin' cops fuck up their careers because they take my money? Not my problem. Not my shit. All my shit, that was tight. I had it all locked down before tonight."

"I came into your building and your boys had been fucked up by the competition already. Me and Munday, we came into your fuckin' house just to kill you. And we got in. I don't give a fuck if the world is ending, man. If you can lose all your shit in one night, you never had shit to begin with.

113

You're a fuckin' bull-shitter. There's a billion out there just like you."

"What you got that's so special, huh?" Dutroux squared his shoulders up and frowned. The blood from his forehead was blinding him in one eye. He spat some blood out of his mouth. "What makes you the shit? Who made you the boss man, motherfucker? You just a cop. You just some punk who couldn't do shit for himself so had to join some bullshit and get the government to give you a badge so you can act like you own shit. You got nothin', you never had nothin', and ain't never gonna have nothin'. You ain't got the fuckin' balls for it."

Barcomb looked down at the rooftop. Ash was watching them. She had a gun in her hand and tears in her eyes.

"I grew up with cops like you," Dutroux said. "Little dicks, all y'all. You gotta beat on kids to make yourselves feel like a man. Shit's turned now, though. Now you the little bitch. Now you runnin' scared. Your whole life - all two fuckin' days of it, I say - you're gonna be runnin'. You ain't never gonna get to Torrento."

Barcomb holstered his Glock and took a step forward as he pulled out his knife.

"Wait" Dutroux said. He took a step back and was about to fall backwards off the clock tower to the street below. He was off balance, falling away from the clock tower. Barcomb reached out and grabbed him by the scruff of his shirt. The only thing keeping him upright and from falling to his death now was Barcomb.

Dutroux was panicked, his bravado disappearing: "You need me!" he shouted. "You need me, man!"

"I don't need you," Barcomb said. "We'll get into that

fortress ourselves, make it ours. Your friend, I'm gonna kill him just for associating' with a son of a bitch like you."

"Listen," Dutroux said. "Listen. This guy Torrento. He's not like me. He's nothing like me."

Barcomb started to loosen his grip on Dutroux's shirt. Dutroux felt himself going back and it scared him.

"No, wait!" Dutroux screamed. He looked down at the ground below and back to Barcomb. "Torrento," he said, "this guy is a big time motherfucker. You know the Columbian cartel guys? They guys who'll kill your entire families you even look at them wrong?"

"He's with the Columbians?"

"No, man! Those guys are the worst motherfuckers on the planet. You fuck with them, you're gone. You fuck with them, you wish you'd never been born. You wish your wife never been born, your kids, your moms, your dad. The Columbians will ruin your life so hard you wish you never had any of it." Dutroux closed his eyes. "But even the Columbians," Dutroux said, opening his eyes again, "are scared of Torrento."

"Bullshit," Barcomb said.

"Listen to me," Dutroux said. "I'd been trying to get this guy's business for years. You wanna know how I finally got it?"

"I'm listening."

"Barcomb, I cut off a cop's head and fuckin' sent it back to them in the mail. I did that to impress Torrento. That's what it takes. That's what he expects. That's who he is."

Barcomb pulled Dutroux forward a second to shift his grip. He grabbed Dutroux and held him now just with a hand clenched around his throat.

Ash burst through onto the rooftop, the door banging hard into the wall. She looked up at the bell tower and saw Barcomb and Dutroux. Barcomb looked down and met her eyes. She was scowling, her face wet with tears. Barcomb looked back to Dutroux.

"Listen to me," Dutroux said, struggling to talk with Barcomb's hand gripping his throat, and he was as sincere as he'd ever said anything in his entire life, "if you go up against Torrento, that's it, man. You are going to get your people killed."

Barcomb shook his head. "I don't think so." He smiled at Dutroux and said, "See you later, motherfucker."

Dutroux's face fell. He knew he was about to die. He knew it before, but now he could feel it. The knowledge took over his whole body and he slumped. For a second he found his strength. He looked Barcomb right in the eyes and said, "You're all gonna die."

Barcomb thrust the knife up into and through Dutroux's ribs with a satisfying crack.

"Not in your lifetime," Barcomb said.

Dutroux looked surprised. His mouth dropped open and his eyes went real wide. His hand gripped Barcomb on the forearm. His other hand dropped his empty gun and it fell down to the street below. Barcomb gutted Dutroux, tearing down towards his waist and opening him up. Barcomb threw the knife on the floor, still holding Dutroux by the throat. He took Haws's grenade from his belt, removed the pin with his teeth, and shoved it inside Dutroux's open torso. Barcomb pulled him back so he was standing upright and then let go of his throat.

"I'm sorry," Dutroux said, unsteady on his feet, tears blinding him.

"Sorry don't get it done," Barcomb said.

Barcomb shoved Dutroux hard and he flew backwards off the clock tower with a high-pitched scream which only stopped when he hit the ground below and the grenade detonated showering a twenty-foot radius in the blood, the brains and the shit of James Dutroux, drug dealer, cop killer.

Barcomb looked down at the mess and sighed.

Chapter 12: Goodbye, Jimmy

What was left of Dutroux was dribbling down the gutter and into the sewer.

Just where he belongs, Barcomb thought.

Barcomb climbed down the stairs to the rooftop. Ash was waiting for him at the door as he stepped out into the cold air of the dawn. The city was turning a golden red as the sun rose. The screams were becoming less and less common, but they were always there. Barcomb, even after one night of Hell, couldn't imagine life now without screams nearby. It weighed on him.

But tossing Dutroux from that tower sure did take a lot of that weight off.

Barcomb saw that it did something to Ash, too.

Ash hugged him tight. She tried to say thank you, but the tears wouldn't stop coming. Barcomb held her. He knew why she was crying. Dutroux was dead, but Dutroux wasn't the end. Her husband, Jimmy, was a dirty cop. Jimmy was her entire world. Jimmy was her life. Jimmy was her future. And Dutroux took that all away. Barcomb hated dirty cops, but Jimmy had a change of heart. Jimmy was OK by him. He wanted to clean himself up, do the right thing and take responsibility for his actions. Dutroux took a machete to Jimmy and Jimmy's head ended up in the Elizabeth P.D. morgue. Ash's long-term future, for the longest time, had become a black hole, an empty void. What used to be there, Dutroux took all that away.

Dutroux took all that away, but a piece of it remained.

Jimmy's head was still in the morgue.

"Let's go," Barcomb said.

He led her by the hand through the building, down through the blood-soaked corridors, over the bodies of the

118

assholes who had tried to fuck with them, past a pile of zombies who had got in, got hungry and tore each other up. It was the first time either of them had seen the destruction in the light of day, and it was like seeing it all for the very first time. Barcomb felt like he'd been through a nightmare and woken up, but it was all still as it was when he was asleep.

The blood looked a little darker than he imagined it was in the night, more purple. The entrails and the organs and the brains, it all looked a little unreal. Maybe it was his mind, helping him cope, or maybe Barcomb had just killed enough last night that it had flipped a switch. If the switch was flipped, he wasn't sure it could be flipped back. In this new world, he wasn't sure he'd want it to be.

The morgue was in the back corner of the building. Barcomb checked his Glock. Good enough, he thought. He opened the door. The cold, steel room echoed with bangs and groans from the refrigerators built into the walls.

"It's OK," Barcomb said. "They're not going anywhere. I know where Jimmy is."

Barcomb went to the last column of refrigerators and pulled the middle drawer. Inside was a plastic black box with a grey lid. It wasn't moving.

Ash searched her belt. She'd lost her knife somewhere along the way. Barcomb handed her his knife and she nodded. Her face had turned stern, unreadable. She'd locked her emotions down as tight as possible. Barcomb knew she'd thought about nothing else since the zombie crisis began. This was a moment she'd been thinking about all night.

"I'll get the lid," Barcomb said.

Ash nodded.

They'd both seen Jimmy's severed head before, back when it was fresh, when it was news. Now his head was something entirely different; it was a demon, something

119

which had haunted both of their dreams. Barcomb had been seeing it every time he closed his eyes. He came with Ash the first time she had to ID the head. It was nothing like this, and he never thought he'd have to do it again.

Barcomb lifted the lid. The head was face down. All he saw in the cold florescent light of the morgue was the back of Jimmy's head. It didn't look like it was moving.

"I don't know that it's come back," Barcomb said.

Ash said nothing. She took a step forward and looked at it. "It's not moving."

"You want me to turn it over?"

"Leave me," Ash said. "I'll handle it."

Barcomb looked at her, but her focus was entirely on her dead husband's severed head. He recalled how he found her in her apartment, cutting the head off the crazy cat lady, just to see if the head survived by itself. That head survived. Ash, as she waited to see if this head re-animated, knew this was going to plague her thoughts, possibly for the rest of her life, however short a time that might be. Barcomb walked over to the door. He looked back at her.

"You sure?" Barcomb said.

She was already lifting the head out of the box by its hair, the knife in her other hand.

Barcomb saw its mouth moving, snapping and wiggling like it was trying to scream and eat all at the same time. He didn't see the eyes. That nightmare was to be Ash's alone. Barcomb stepped outside and closed the door behind him. He heard muffled last words and the crunch of a knife through a skull. A minute later, Ash opened the door and walked past him without a second word.

Chapter 13: Goodbye, Elizabeth

Barcomb had lived in Elizabeth all his life. It had never been an easy relationship. She had given him a pretty rough ride at times. She could be a real bitch. The town had no visitors, no real tourists, only drug runners and people who took a wrong turn on the way to New York. But Barcomb knew her well enough to know her good side. He saw parts of Elizabeth very few people got to see. He had seen the absolute worst of the worst. He had seen things so terrible he couldn't even have imagined them, things that still woke him up in the middle of long, winter nights covered in sweat. Elizabeth was home to idiots, to maniacs, to psychopaths, to the poor and the desperate. It was a stage on which every disgusting act known to man had been performed. Usually at three in the morning around the back of Barcomb's house from the sounds of what his neighbors were up to. But, despite everything, Elizabeth still had people who cared. Elizabeth still had a real community. Elizabeth was beautiful in her own way.

Barcomb, Haws and Ash stood beside the Humvee on top of the hillside overlooking the town. None of them could speak. Barcomb knew, looking down, that all of that was gone now. There was no more beauty, no more community, no nothing. There was life and there was death, and things they were gonna have to do to stay alive, he thought, some of those might even be worse than death.

Munday lay in the back of the Humvee asleep, trying to recover, her mind trying to forget.

Barcomb tried tightening the makeshift bandage around his head to stop it from falling over his eyes, but it just shifted down. Ash moved his hands away and tightened it for him. He nodded his thanks and she smiled at him. Her smile faded when she looked back to Elizabeth below as the red glow of the dawn crept between the buildings towards them. It had been only a few nights since the sickness took hold, but already Elizabeth was beyond saving. There was no coming back from this. Too many lives had been lost. Too many zombies had torn too many friends and family apart. A lot of people, their entire lives, the whole support structure of people they knew, now lay rotting in the street. And too many people had done things they could never come back from. Society had broken down entirely, and it only took a few days. Barcomb realized how fragile it must have been before, how precious.

He finally found his voice.

"We'll be back," he said, not sure if he believed it.

Ash nodded.

"You know it, brother," Haws said.

"We'll head to the hills, find this Torrento fuck, take whatever he has and regroup. New Providence," Barcomb said. "After that, we take back the city. Nobody's coming to save us. Nobody's coming to help us. Elizabeth isn't on the radar of anyone important, so unless we do it ourselves, it ain't getting done."

"We're gonna need more people," Ash said. "You can't rely on me to keep saving your sorry asses."

"We'll find help," Barcomb said. "There has to be more survivors who got out of the city. We still got Buddy and a shitload of guns, and we're a Hell of a team. Munday'll be back on her feet soon. She's gotta be. Then we go."

"What's the plan, bro?" Haws said. "What's the end game here?"

"Plan is we take on Torrento, shore up the house, tool up, head back in, and slaughter every last one of those fuckin' beasts. End game is being alive, retaking Elizabeth, and having a few fuckin' beers."

Haws nodded. They all looked down at the destroyed city in the light of day.

"We'll be back," Barcomb said. "Just you fuckin' see if we aren't."

TO BE CONTINUED

Officer Barcomb
VS
The Undead
Part 2

Chapter 1: No Escape

Don't panic, she thought. Stay calm. You'll find them. They're here somewhere. Don't panic.

Officer Rachel Munday pushed her wet hair away from her eyes as she stumbled between the trees and through the pouring rain with a small flashlight and a Glock holding only two bullets. She couldn't see more than a couple feet in front of her face. All she could hear was the roar of the wind and the rain and the faint screams of the undead lurking somewhere in the darkness. Her heavy boots sank in the mud. She was miles from home and stranded in unfamiliar woodland as the water rose around her. Her clothes were soaked through. She was numb with cold and trembling in fear. The wood was becoming a swamp and the storm was becoming a flash flood. This day was quickly looking like it may be her last.

"Barcomb!" she shouted. "Barcomb!"

The pine trees towered above her. They groaned in the wind and blocked out the moonlight. They funneled the rain directly down into the dirt, creating a slush which made walking hard and running impossible. The muscles in her legs burned with the effort.

"Barcomb!" she shouted, becoming desperate. "Haws! Where the fuck are you?"

Her eyes were tearing up and she could feel her lip quivering. In her head she heard the voices of every man who'd ever told her she wasn't cut out for police work. She heard them laugh behind her back again. With her long, blonde hair and beach bunny physique, it took a long time to win them over. She still wasn't sure she ever had. She'd stopped drinking after work because there'd always be some

guy at the bar - doesn't matter whether he was green out of
the academy or a lieutenant with a wife, two kids and a
spaniel waiting for him at home – and she'd spend an hour
fending him off before she got sick of the staring and the
leering and went home. She wasn't gonna be anyone's trophy
fuck and she worked her ass off to get to the strike team, to
Barcomb's strike team.

Where is he?

The sky growled with thunder and lit up in a blinding
flash and Munday winced. She thought she saw a figure up
ahead between the trees. It was three hours since the group
had been split up. They stopped for gas at a service station
next to a freeway and looked around. The place was blown all
to Hell. There were corpses scattered all over the place, cars
had rolled onto their roofs and gas had leaked all over the
forecourt. It was risky, but without gas they were as good as
dead. The zombies were fast, so they knew you were on
borrowed time if you're walking around on foot, especially if
you're carrying supplies on your back. They found a working
pump and were halfway done when a horde of zombies
descended on them from every direction. The world had
gotten real quiet since the end. That's what they'd started
calling it now: the end. It wasn't a crisis. It wasn't a disaster. It
was the end of everything. And when the world is silent, any
movement, any noise, it draws attention. Attention, in this
new world, always meant a fight.

Munday couldn't see the figure up ahead anymore
when she tried to squint through the rain and the darkness.
Maybe it's Barcomb, she thought. She didn't dare think about
what it meant if it wasn't him. She didn't have the bullets for
anything else and she'd already started thinking about saving a
bullet for herself. If she ran into a horde, if she got cornered
right now, she wasn't sure she wouldn't end it right there. She
was tough. She was only 26 years old, but those years had

tested her, matured her. After growing up in Oklahoma City, just her and a drunk, mentally ill dad, Munday felt she could take anything life could throw at her. Those times still hurt her when they came to mind, but she had been grateful for them, for the strong person they'd made her into. She knew a lot of women her age, girls from the neighborhood, who were soft. They'd surrendered early. They never really wanted anything, so they settled for what they were given by the men in their lives. Munday promised herself she would never be like that. She would never depend on a man again. She'd never owe anyone anything.

Now she needed Barcomb and, after he rescued her from Dutroux and his men, she owed him her life. Dutroux and the other men took everything from her. They broke her down. They took turns with her. Dutroux had his turn. Even Duke - that dumb college kid they rescued from a locked cage in the back of a supermarket - even he had a turn. Munday didn't know where he got to afterwards. Nobody did. She thought about him every day, but not about what he did to her. It wasn't what they did that she remembered – she was so badly beaten that a lot of it was a blur – it was how she felt that would haunt her. She wanted to die. More than anything, she didn't want to live in this world. She fought and fought until they beat it out of her. They treated her like a piece of meat, and, after everything, that's how she felt, like a wounded animal that needed to be destroyed for its own good. She fought the urge to end it even after Barcomb, Haws and Ash rescued her. She fought it every day. When she got scared, it got worse. And she was real scared right now.

Where is he? She thought.

Despite everything, there was something inside her, some driving force – maybe her father's face – that made her want to live. That man had destroyed her childhood, almost ruined her life, and she claimed it back, made something of herself. She was proud of the woman she'd become. She'd be damned if a man like Dutroux would take that from her.

She heard the guttural cry of a zombie nearby. It drew her out of her thoughts and back into the world. She felt sick with fear and she focused on that sickness. It was there for a reason: she needed to be afraid; she needed to stay sharp. A cracking sound came from behind her.

Munday turned and saw a zombie falling to the ground near her feet. Its legs cracked again and the bones split as they buckled under the weight of moving too quickly. It was excited. It snarled and snapped, showing no pain as its shins splintered beneath it and its cold, rotten muscles were shredded by the bone fragments. Its hands grasped air as it reached for her. It grunted and groaned. When it snapped its jaws again, some of its teeth buckled and popped out under the pressure of its enthusiasm.

"Fuck!" Munday said, falling backwards in her hurry to get away.

Her ass hit the ground hard and she scrambled back with her hands. Her Glock went into the mud, the barrel jamming up with it. She lifted it and tried to fire, but nothing happened. The zombie kept coming until its foot was caught in a fallen branch. It clawed forward until its decaying foot detached at the ankle with a sickening ripping noise. Munday kicked its head, snapping its neck. It kept coming, its head now tilted at an inhuman angle and its dried, yellowing eyes looking right at her, right into her eyes. It didn't want meat. It wanted to destroy her. It looked at her as a person, not a meal. Its eyes were nearly dropping out of its head, but Munday had never seen such pure hatred. Not since she was a kid. It was dressed in blood- and shit-soaked shirt and trousers, like her father used to wear.

The zombie's ice-cold hands grabbed her legs and it pulled itself up. The smell made her almost gag immediately. She punched it in the head and pieces of its hair and scalp came off against her fist.

"Fuck off!" Munday screamed.

Its bony fingers dug into her body as it crawled on top of her. She hit its head with the butt of her Glock and it kept coming for her with its broken neck putting its head at a curious angle. She heard its skull crack under the blows, but it wouldn't stop.

Its mouth was over her face. She held it back with a hand on its neck, but she could feel the flesh giving way underneath. It was like trying to hold onto Jell-O. She could even feel its bones beneath the skin and rotted muscle in its neck. It snapped its jaws again and Munday could feel it's cold breath; she could smell the rotting state of its internal organs. She tried to push it off, but its rage made it strong. She tried to pistol-whip it again, but it didn't die. Instead, it just broke its neck more, moving its head closer to her face. The next bite would reach her.

It lunged.

Munday shoved the barrel of her Glock sideways between its teeth. It bit down and shook its head, like a crocodile trying to paralyze its prey. Two more teeth broke off in its black gums. Munday's mind was sinking in despair. This was the end. She was going to die trapped in the mud and the rain and no-one would ever find her.
This is it, she thought.

The zombie's hands were on her head, grabbing her face and pulling at her hair. Its open mouth struggled against the barrel of the Glock. The noise was animalistic, like a starved pig dancing for joy at the sight of a full trough. It drooled and the grey slime that poured from its mouth soaked the gun and dripped onto Munday's face. She felt it dribbling into her own mouth and she spat. All she could think about was death. And, then, for just a moment, she thought about life, about living, about what that would mean. It was only a passing thought, but it was enough to move her to action. She made a fist and punched as hard as she could under the zombie's jaw. Its teeth completely shattered. Munday grabbed its lower jaw from the inside and tore it off, throwing it aside. The zombie became frantic but it no longer had anything with which to bite. Munday let go of its head and it tried to bite her, rubbing its black tongue and the open wound where its mouth used to be against her cheek. The slime it left on her face was cold and sticky. Munday dropped her gun and grabbed its head either side with both hands. She twisted it right around and felt the spine give way. She turned it three times completely around as its tongue flapped and it made hideous screeching sounds. After the three turns, she yanked it hard and pulled the entire head free from its neck with a burst of stale blood that covered her. With that, the body stopped moving.

Munday stood and took the still-moving head and placed it on the ground. She stamped, hard, and it popped like a watermelon under her boot.

She stood and looked up at the darkness between the trees, letting the rain wash the slime and blood from her face as she caught her breath. She then screamed at the top of her lungs: "Barcomb! Where are you?"

When Munday put her face in her hands, she felt something, a pain. She took her hand away from her face and there was blood on her fingers, fresh blood. She felt her cheek in a panic, already telling herself it was nothing and that she would be OK. She felt the sting again when she pressed her cheek and she knew, then, that should would never be OK again.

She was bit.

It must have scratched my face with a broken tooth, she thought. Maybe that doesn't count. Maybe that's not a real bite.

The radio had been on and off in the time since the end, but it was very clear about one thing: bites mean a slow death and a quick resurrection; bites mean infection.

She had an open cut on her face and it had been covered in spit and slime and blood. She knew in her heart she was infected. Maybe she was lucky and nothing got into her bloodstream, but deep down she could feel it. She felt dirty. She felt infected. She would die soon. Munday picked up her gun and cleaned the mud from the barrel.

She thought about ending it there with a bullet through the head.

That was another tip from the radio: kill the brain; nothing else works.

She didn't want to become one of those things.

Munday checked her ammo for the hundredth time and there were still two bullets. She lifted her Glock and put the barrel under her chin. She thought, and then adjusted it, seeing the bullet's trajectory in her mind's eye. She was almost blind with tears. She sobbed uncontrollably. Everything she ever was, everything she ever overcame, it would end in the dark in the middle of nowhere with nobody around to give a shit. She moved the barrel to her temple. Cleaner shot, she thought. Maybe less painful. More direct to the brain.

26 years old and that was her lot. Plenty of people had been cut short recently, but it didn't make her any more grateful for what she'd had. She wanted more. She imagined everyone who wanted to die wanted the same thing. That didn't make it hurt any less.

She placed her finger on the trigger and tried to memorize her last experience of this world: it was wet, cold, frightening and painful. She heard a sound and it prompted a new thought. It was the sound of a car. She thought about sticking around. She might be lucky. It might not be infected. The sound of car grew louder and she saw lights in the distance. I might live, she thought. There's a chance I'm not infected.

She ran down to get in front of the car. There must be a road there, she thought.

And by the time her boots hit the asphalt, she had convinced herself completely that she was not infected.

She stood directly in the middle of the road and waved her arms in the air, the Glock in one hand and a flashlight in the other. She waved the beam of her flashlight towards the windshield of the oncoming car. It was coming fast. Munday was smiling. The closer the car got without slowing down, the faster Munday's smile disappeared.

"Stop!" she screamed.

The car kept coming. It was bearing down on her fast. She was directly in its path.

"Please!" she screamed, louder.

It was a small car, a sedan. The lights were bright. Looking around, she saw zombies in the woods on the other side of the road from which she had come. They were noticing her now that she was screaming and waving her flashlight. She got tired and she lowered her arms. She looked at the oncoming car helplessly.

"Please," she muttered.

The car was almost on top of her when she raised her Glock and fired her last two rounds into the windshield. The car swerved suddenly and span wildly out of control. It hit the embankment and was thrown into the air, landing on its roof with a crash that every zombie for miles around would have heard.

Munday was devastated. The car was undriveable now. Its roof had buckled in and one of the wheels had twisted on the axel. Gas leaked from the fuel tank. Steam rose from the front end. She heard no movement inside as she approached.

She needed to be quick. Zombies were no doubt on their way. But she needed ammo. Maybe there was some in the car. Anything would do. She saw an assault rifle lying on the road near the car and her heart bounced with joy.

It was an AR-15.

When she kneeled beside the driver's window to look for a box of ammo, she saw the driver.

"No," she said. "Please, God, no."

It was Barcomb. He'd been shot in the chest and head.

Chapter 2: 911

This zombie was different. There was something about it Ash didn't like. She studied it closely from her position up a tree in a half-built tree house full of soggy comic books and empty Coke bottles. It wore a blood-splattered fireman's outfit, helmet and all, and held a fire axe dangling from one hand. The axe had chunks of flesh clinging to it. The zombie didn't move. It stood almost completely still, grunting and groaning. It stared at the ground.

"What's it doing?" Haws whispered.

"It's just... standing there," Ash whispered back.

"Is it listening?"

"I don't know."

It was a little cramped in the rickety children's tree house for Ash, being up there with Haws, a mountain of a man with cropped blonde hair, stubble and a motorcycle jacket over a dirty t-shirt. Ash was half his size with her long black hair tied back and her slender physique, half of which was on show due to various rips and tears to her jeans, vest top and hunting jacket combo. It had been a rough couple of weeks since the world went to Hell in a hand basket.

"Shall I take care of it?" Haws said, holding up a tactical shotgun. "I got three rounds left."

Ash shook her head. "We can't afford the noise."

Haws pulled out his radio and whispered into it, "Barcomb, where are you, brother?"

"Anything?" Ash said.

Haws shook his head.

Another zombie ambled through the dark forest and came close to their tree. Because of the rain, Ash couldn't see it right away. The fireman seemed to notice it much earlier and became agitated, wandering backwards and forwards. The zombie intruder was a naked elderly man, stumbling in the wet mud, falling and getting up, moaning, presumably, in frustration. The skin on the right side of its face was slipping away from the greening muscle tissue beneath. Its lower lip had sunk to reveal rotten teeth covered in strips of dirty meat from his last meal. One eyeball was dry and punctured, the other flitting around constantly. Ash and Haws watched, curious as to what they would do to each other. They had seen zombies attack one another before when they ran out of living meat. They'd eat anything.

The fireman zombie lifted its axe and swung with force, clumsily but in the right direction. The axe landed in the other zombie's chest, breaking through it and coming out from the side, making the elderly zombie lurch to one side and then fall down as the contents of its upper torso hit the forest floor.

"Fuck me," Haws said.

Ash looked at him.

"They can use weapons?" Haws said.

They watched as the elderly zombie writhed on the floor to get back up, its arms now twisted and in the wrong place now that the torso was split almost in two. The firefighter then did something even stranger. It watched. It looked down with the axe in its hand at the wriggling zombie. It swung the axe down again.

"What the fuck is it doing?" Haws said.

The firefighter pulled the axe out, with pieces of rotten lungs attached. The elderly zombie still struggled and tried to get up. The firefighter peered from under its bright yellow helmet with dry eyeballs and half of its face burned away to expose the bone beneath. The firefighter swung the axe down again.

"It's not trying to eat it," Ash said. "It's trying to kill it."

The firefighter's axe severed the elderly zombie's right shoulder completely from its torso. When the senior zombie continued struggling and grunting and trying to get up, the firefighter looked at it and tilted its head like a curious dog.

The firefighter swung the axe down into the elderly zombie's head and it died.

"Oh, my fucking shit," Ash said.

"What the..." Haws said.

Ash's face was white. "It killed it."

"You look like you've seen a ghost," Haws said. "It's fucked up, but-"

"Do you know what this means?" Ash said. "Haws, that thing down there, it just learned from its mistakes."

Haws frowned, confused.

"These zombies," Ash said, "they can learn. They're dumb, but they get smarter."

"What does that mean?" Haws said.

"It means they're only gonna get harder to kill."

Haws leaned forward to take a better look at the undead firefighter. The board beneath his hand broke off and Haws tumbled forward.

"Fuck!" Haws shouted.

Ash grabbed him by his belt and stopped him falling. Haws reached back and pulled himself back fully onto the half-built tree house.

"That was fuckin' close," he said, laughing.

Ash smiled, and then looked down to the ground.

The firefighter was looking right at them.

"We may be in some trouble," Ash said.

"We'll be fine. What can he do from down there?" Haws said.

The firefighter moved slowly towards the base of the tree. He looked up. They were more than 50 feet up. Haws spat over the edge and it bounced off the zombie's helmet.

"Nice hat, asshole," Haws said with a grin. "Let's see you climb this shit."

The firefighter looked at the bloodied axe it was holding for a few moments. Its face was blank. Ash watched it carefully, shielding her eyes from the rain with her hands. The firefighter lifted the axe up at his side.

137

The zombie firefighter went to work at chopping down the tree.

"Holy fuckin' shit," Haws said.

The axe wasn't having much effect, chipping only a small amount of wood away at a time, but it was slowly working. More than that, however, was the sound of it. Knock. Knock. Knock. Ash and Haws watched helplessly as the sound echoed through the forest and dark figures started limping out of the darkness towards their tree.

"That sound is gonna get us both killed," Ash said, "never mind the axe. He's ringing the goddamn dinner bell."

Haws nodded and said, "We may be in some trouble."

Ash grabbed the radio from Haws's hand and spoke into it. "Barcomb, if you're out there," she said, "now would be a really great fuckin' time to ride in and rescue us."

Chapter 3: Patrol Dog

The rain wasn't letting up. Munday was soaked through to her very bones. She removed her jacket and placed it under Barcomb's head. He was breathing, but he was unconscious. Blood pooled around the wound on his chest, just above the heart. Munday had laid him on the ground under a large bush, somewhat hidden from view. There wasn't enough room for her, however, so she was a sitting duck. The car was on its roof. The road was deserted apart from a few corpses lying face down on the asphalt with various parts bitten or torn off. Rain water was streaming down the slight hillside, carrying soil from the forest onto the road. Munday was at a loss for what to do next. She hugged the AR-15 close and prayed nothing would get close enough that she'd have to use it. They couldn't afford the attention.

Underneath the constant swish of the rain, she started to hear moaning.

They're coming, she thought. They're coming whether I like it or not.

Munday stood up and looked around. She took Barcomb's knife from his belt and cut length of cloth from her pants. She squeezed it dry and took out a lighter from her pocket.

If they're coming anyway, she thought, let's try and get someone else here, too. I got a big fuckin' sign over my head right now anyway after that crash.

Munday dabbed the cloth in gasoline that was pooled under the car, then opened the fuel cap and jammed the cloth inside. She took out a lighter and, shielding it with her hands; she set fire to the cloth. She couldn't move right away. The rain would put out the cloth. She needed to stay to make sure that didn't happen, but too long and she'd be blown all to Hell. She decided to count to twenty, whatever happened.

She closed her eyes.

This is a long shot, she thought. This is so fuckin' stupid. I'm getting myself killed. This is insane.

And then, in the darkness behind her eyes and for what seemed like an eternity, she thought only of the numbers between twenty and one as she felt the warmth of the flames beneath her hands. She tried to imagine she was warming her hands on her grandmother's fire, a cup of coffee and a warm snack waiting for her when she was done.

The heat on her hands was becoming unbearable.

Munday opened her eyes. Three zombies were bearing down on her from the side of the road. The flames were higher in the tank. She turned and ran. When she got close to the other side of the road, there was a deafening boom and a wall of heat punched her in the back and sent her flying to the ground. A zombie landed around her. Although the parts would have formed one complete zombie, they were mixed limbs and flesh from the three. Munday pushed herself up and tore a fragment of steel from her forearm. The heat on her back from the fire was almost unbearable. She touched the scratch on her cheek. There was a moment's doubt, but she told herself once again that she was lucky, that she wasn't infected.

She went back over to Barcomb.

"You want to get me killed," came a gruff voice from under the bush, "you could stop fucking about and just shoot me again."

Barcomb sat up slowly, holding his chest in agony. Munday helped him stand. Barcomb looked at the burning car.

"Please tell me you took out the crate of beer that was in the back before you decided to set the car on fire," Barcomb said.

"There was beer in there?" Munday said.

Barcomb nodded. He started to fall and Munday caught him. "You have to take it easy," she said.

"I'll take it easy when I'm dead," Barcomb quipped.

"No, you won't. You'll be running around screaming and eating people like the rest of those crazy zombie bastards."

Barcomb touched the wound on his chest and the other on his head which was a huge gash just above his eye that left a small flap of skin hanging off and his right eye covered in sticky blood. His chest wouldn't stop bleeding. He applied pressure.

"I thought you were dead," Munday said. "I thought I'd killed you."

"You'll have to try harder next time."

"I shot you twice and you flipped your car. I might just have to give up on the whole idea."

"About that…" Barcomb said.

Munday looked around as the trees along the side of the road started rustling and the night came alive with grunting and guttural shrieking. Barcomb nodded down the road.

"Excuses will have to wait, I guess," he said.

"Can you walk?"

"More or less." Barcomb saw the AR-15 on her shoulder. "Give me my gun."

He took the AR-15 and handed her a clip for her Glock.

"What was the plan with the fire anyway?"

"Distress call," Munday said.

"Well, you seem to have just called in more distress."

"You know where Haws and Ash are?"

Barcomb shook his head. "Got separated after the attack on the Humvee."

They walked quickly down the road. Barcomb was unsteady, but not slow. Every step caused him almost unbearable pain. He tore off a piece of his shirt and stuck in his mouth to bite down.

"After that, I booked it to the nearest house to regroup," he said, muffled through the cloth. "Seemed like everyone else went the other way, so I stole a car."

"Was the house safe?"

Barcomb shook his head. "Overrun. No windows left. There was a swimming pool. It was red."

"Do you think Dutroux was lying about the whole thing, everything about the big house with the big walls and the supplies? Or do you think he just lied about where it was?"

"I don't know."

"Do you think this Torrento guy really exists?"

"I never heard of him," Barcomb said. "So either he's bullshit or he's the sneakiest motherfucker alive."

Barcomb looked forward and stopped. Munday was looking at him and carried on for a moment. Then she turned and saw what he saw. Dozens of zombies were coming towards them, their hands outstretched, their mouths snarling.

"We don't have the ammo for this," Munday said.

"I don't have the legs to run," Barcomb said.

Munday looked at Barcomb.

"If you're waiting for me to tell you to save yourself and leave me behind," Barcomb said, "you're in for a long fuckin' wait."

Barcomb checked his mag and frowned. He nearly fell down and righted himself. Munday had a full clip, but it still wouldn't be enough. Barcomb looked over his shoulder towards the burning wreck and more zombies were coming from that direction, running first through the fire and then towards him and Munday after they spotted them down the road. Seven or eight burning zombies were ambling towards them from one direction and five times as many were running and walking from the other.

Barcomb remembered his radio. He picked it up to speak into it.

The radio was smashed.

"Shit," he said.

The zombies were closing fast.

"Into the woods," Barcomb said. "Now!"

They hit the darkness beyond the trees. Barcomb tumbled into the wet mud. He pulled himself out, regained his breath and shut his eyes for a moment.

"Maybe they don't see so good," Barcomb said, looking at Munday again. "Their eyes should be all fucked up, anyway."

"Maybe-" Munday began, before an almighty bang sounded and the zombies screeched in chorus and the roar of a six-wheeler truck drowned them out.

Bodies exploded into goopy red clouds with the crunch of bones and the slap of meat as the truck plowed through the crowd, throwing flesh and strings of blood and intestines into the air. The truck slammed onto its brakes with a scraping sound and skidded to a stop on the insides of a dozen zombies, right beside the burning car. For a moment it just sat there with no movement inside. Barcomb and Munday exchanged a nervous glance.

The truck was without a trailer. It was metallic blue with a photorealistic supermodel in a red bikini spray-painted

144

on the side. A terminator skeleton was spray-painted on the back. The truck door opened and a man stepped out from behind the wheel. He was dressed in a shirt and tie. He didn't look much like a truck driver to Barcomb. The driver looked around. He leaned into the cab and grabbed the radio.

"No sign of anyone," he said into it. "Must all be dead. I'll look around for anything useful and kill anything that moves."

"You see any good meat," a deep Jamaican voice said, "you be a good boy and bring that on back home, you dig?"

"I'll get the hound on it," the driver said, laughing.

Barcomb frowned and raised his assault rifle, ready for anything. It was heavier than the last time he lifted it. He could feel his strength leaving him.

The driver walked around to the other side of the truck and opened the door. Munday could see under the truck where another person climbed down. The strange thing was, she saw hands touch the floor first, not feet. The feet came down after. She heard a loud bark and her face scrunched up, confused, instinctively disgusted.

The driver walked back around and Munday and Barcomb got a look at his "hound". The hound was a naked woman in her early 20s with dark hair which had been scruffily cut short, with a knife from the looks of it. Her knees and elbows were red raw and she was painfully thin, looking almost starved with her bones clearly visible poking through her skin. She panted like a dog as she walked on all fours. She barked.

Barcomb whispered, "What in the name of fuckin' shit is that?"

145

Munday was silent. Munday was furious. She fought every urge to run out and start shooting at the driver as he smiled at his hound and patted her on the head. He kneeled beside her and grabbed her face to make her look at him. He said something to her and she started running off towards the trees in the other direction on all fours, panting and barking.

Barcomb pointed back into the dark forest and Munday understood: time to get the fuck out of there before shit gets weird.

Weird-*er*.

Barcomb and Munday hiked through the woods, taking it slow, trying to stay quiet and struggling to navigate through only by moonlight. Munday led the way, though she didn't know where they could go. Barcomb's wounds slowed him down, made him careless. He stood on branches and they cracked beneath his boots.

It was around ten minutes later when they heard bizarre fake growling in front of them. The driver's human dog walked into the moonlight on all fours. She snarled. Munday and Barcomb trained their guns on the insane, naked woman in front of them.

"We must've walked in a circle," Barcomb said, wiping the rain from his eyes with the sleeve of his shirt as he trained his gun on the "dog". "Fuck's sake," he said.

"What the fuck is it?" Munday said.

"This is some dark shit," Barcomb said. "I don't even wanna know."

Then they heard the click of the hammer on a pistol being drawn back. It came from behind them. Then there came a voice: "Don't do anything stupid, now," the driver said. "I'd love nothing more than to kill the pair of you, loot your shit and fuck your corpses, so if you want to make me the happiest man alive you just hang onto those guns and see how it goes for you."

Barcomb and Munday placed their weapons on the ground and got on their knees.

Barcomb was bleeding.

He was bleeding badly.

The "dog" barked at them. It snarled and showed teeth which had been filed into crude points, into sharp fangs.

Chapter 4: Death's Door

"You call that dancing'?" he said. "Put your fuckin' back into it. Fuck we keep you around here for? Might as well throw you to the fuckin' goons outside and let them chew you up."

Shannon had heard that they called him "Beat" after some movie star or other because he was Japanese. Or half-Japanese, at least. He didn't look Asian. Maybe that was the joke. He sat there in his boxers watching her shake her ass in a bikini that was two sizes too small. He had short blonde hair, light blue eyes, and his chest was waxed and hairless and his shoulders were the size of a gorilla's. Shannon had no doubt that he could snap her neck with one squeeze. That's why she danced. Beat had been sizing her up for a while. If she could get on his good side, she might be allowed to stay. She might even be given real food, real meals. Since the start of all the death and insanity, she'd barely eaten enough to keep her on her feet.

It'll be over soon, she thought. I just need to keep going a couple more weeks and everything will get back to normal. I can go back to working as a teaching assistant. I can see my boyfriend again, wherever he might be now. I'll find her parents and everything can be back to how it was. It can't be as bad as it looks, she thought. Things don't go that bad that fast. The TV was wrong. It hadn't been broadcasting for a few days, but it must be wrong. This isn't so bad. They're exaggerating. The world isn't that cruel. Things will be OK. They always are.

They *have* to be.

"Come here," Beat said, waving her over with an enormous, pale hand. He put it on her waist. His hand was so cold she jumped. "What're you afraid of?" he said. "I'm not gonna hurt you."

Shannon tried not to look around the room at the trophies of the other girls who had let Beat down. There were locks of hair in jars, pieces of jewelry, a clean skull from which all the flesh had been boiled and peeled off. She counted over two dozen trophies; she understood this was not a new personality trait for this rhinoceros of a man. He was like this before everything happened. But all these trophies were fresh. She was terrified, but if she showed even a trace of it he would get turned off.

That was the fastest way to make her way onto his trophy shelf.

Turning around, she backed up into his crotch, rubbing her ass against him. She could hear him catch his breath. She was onto a winner.

The door burst open.

"We got bad fuckin' news!" It was Franky, one of Beat's regular hook-up girls.

Beat pushed Shannon away and she landed hard on the tiled flooring, her elbows searing with pain.

"He's back!" Franky said.

"He's supposed to be in South America!" Beat said. His face had turned pale. Shannon had never seen a man so big look so goddamn scared. He started pacing and looked out of the ceiling to floor windows. "Shit!" he said. "He's not gonna be happy. He's gonna be far from fuckin' happy. The guys cleared him out, took all his cash, all his supply."

"We can tell him we tried to stop them," Franky said.

149

Beat shook his head. "He'll tell us we failed."

"Well, what the fuck are we supposed to do?"

"We have to kill him," Beat said. He grabbed a handgun from off the coffee table.

"Are you fuckin' nuts?" Franky said. "Have you seen his guys? Boris is with him. You don't kill Boris."

"I can do it. If we kill him, his men will back off. We'll be in charge."

"We can't. You can't kill him."

"What, you in love with him or something? After all the shit you seen him do?"

"Shut the hell up," Franky said, punching him on the shoulder. "We just fuckin' can't. He ain't the kinda man who just dies because you fuckin' want him to!"

Shannon started to stand up when she heard a deafening bang. Without quite knowing why she wanted to, she found herself slowly lying back down on the floor. She felt very tired all of a sudden. She felt tired and warm and when she looked down at the white tiles beneath her, she saw that they were slowly being hidden by a pool of dark red blood. Looking down, she saw that the blood was coming from a hole in her stomach.

Oh, she thought. That's not a great sign.

Shannon was utterly calm for a moment, just observing her blood flooding out onto the floor around her. She felt her breathing getting shallower and could hear these strange little squeaking sounds. The squeaks were coming

150

from her own mouth, and they repeated, becoming louder until they became screams.

Shannon didn't quite understand why she was screaming, but she knew she had to do it.

"Oh, fuckin' shut up," Franky said, grabbing Beat's gun and shooting Shannon again in the back.

The pain was unbearable and it sent Shannon into complete lock down. She could hear and she could see, but she couldn't move and she couldn't control her body. She lay there, looking at the blood pooling around her on the floor, silent now and listening.

She heard a door open and several men with heavy boots entered. Then a man with lighter shoes came in. His shoes sounded pointed, expensive, and he moved slowly. When he spoke, he sounded different. He spoke as slowly as he moved and there was a trace of an accent. Shannon had divorced her mind from her body by this point and felt no pain. She observed. Her own being was not part of her observations.

Middle Eastern, she thought. He sounds like he's from Iraq or something.

"Put down the gun," he said, almost gently.

"I put down the gun and you're gonna kill me, man," Beat said.

"You tell your guys to put down your fuckin' guns," Franky said.

"What's your name?" the Iraqi man said.

151

"Fr-Franky."

"You're a good-looking girl," the Iraqi said. "I always have room for good-looking girls in my villa."

"Look," Beat said. "I worked for you a long time. I'm loyal. I didn't know you were coming back."

"So you rape and kill my women? You allow people to steal my possessions?" the Iraqi screamed. "This is how you work for me? This is loyalty?"

"You move and I'm gonna blow your fuckin' head right off," Franky said.

"I don't know you," the Iraqi said. "And you clearly don't know me."

"I know you'll be the first one to die if anything happens."

Shannon's world was fading fast. Her vision was failing her. The last thing she ever saw was the moonlight shining off her freshly spilled blood. She lay there then, listening, holding on with no real panic, no real despair. Shannon felt as if she was simply falling asleep. It reminded her of her parents' long conversations during car rides when she was a kid. She'd doze and catch bits and pieces and never really try to understand what was being said; she'd just enjoy the sounds they made and let them lull her into sleep.

The Iraqi man spoke again. Shannon didn't catch it. She tuned back in later and heard him say, "The first one of you to kill the other, I will forgive completely. There will be no repercussions. You have worked for me, Beat," he said. "When someone points a gun at me, their life is forfeit. This is a once in a lifetime deal."

There was a long pause, panicked breathing.

The Iraqi sounded calm: "I have five men. Either one of you kills the other, or my men kill both of you."

"You'll die, too," Franky said.

"Do you know my story, little girl?" the Iraqi said. "Do you know where I grew up?

Franky was silent.

"You look beyond these walls and see death and hardship and the end of the world and you quake in your little boots," the Iraqi said, with an eerie calmness. "You see bodies on the streets and hear gunfire wherever you go. You see dead women and children with the flesh stripped from their bones and you ask, 'Where is God?' For me, I look out at burning buildings and I smell burning bodies and I am reminded of home. Where I grew up, children did not live long. Your country cut off our food supply for decades. When a mother and a child came close to death, when they were starved down to the very bones, the mother would find a neighboring family who were also knocking on death's door and she would arrange a trade. Do you know what she would say to her neighbor?"

No-one spoke.

"Your arm is getting tired pointing that gun at me," the Iraqi said, sounding like he was smiling. "Well, let me stop talking in fictions about people without names. I will tell you what my mother said to her neighbor. I was ten years old. My brother was three. I had never and have never again been so hungry in my entire life. That kind of hunger, it sharpens the mind. It prepares you for anything. My mother took my three

153

year old brother – Rizwan was his name – and she spoke with her neighbor, the father of my very best friend, and this is what she said to him: 'You take my child. Kill my youngest son and eat him. And I will do the same to yours.' Few children made it past ten years old. For the parents, for my mother, she could either allow herself and her family to die or she could lose one and perhaps have more children later. I survived," the Iraqi said, "only because I ate the flesh of my best friend. Like the rest of the children of Baghdad, I was not expected to live beyond my tenth birthday. Everything after that is a gift, and I will never again allow an American to dictate terms to me. One of you will die or both of you will. Those are my terms."

Shannon drifted away as Franky started to speak.

She came back when gunfire jolted her back to consciousness. It was a single shot followed by the sound of a body hitting the floor.

"You have regained your honor," the Iraqi said.

"I'm so sorry, Mr. Torrento," Beat said. "It was all her. I didn't want to-"

There was second gunshot and another body hit the floor.

Shannon must have moved, because suddenly she heard someone standing over her, saying "This one's still alive."

There was the sound of pointed, expensive shoes clicking over towards her. Torrento, that was what Beat called him.

"I don't know this woman," Torrento said.

154

Shannon tried to open her eyes. Small rays of light poked through and she could make out shapes, but little else. Still, she was grateful for one last look at the world.

"Cut her up and feed her to the dogs," Torrento said. "These two, I want their heads on sticks on my wall by morning."

Shannon could hear Torrento walking away. He stopped near the door.

"And don't kill their brains," Torrento said. "I want their heads to live up there for a very long time. Put them up next to all the others."

Shannon felt a warm hand on her head, pushing through her hair. Sense memory kicked in and she found herself dozing on a comfortable sofa with her head resting on an old boyfriend's lap as he stroked her hair and talked about plans for the weekend. Life was easy and they had a lot to look forward to.

The hand grabbed a fistful of Shannon's hair and pulled it back.

There was no pain as the blade of a knife drew a line from one side of her exposed throat to the other, opening it up and releasing what little blood she had left onto the floor.

Shannon's last thought, as with most people, was an incoherent, jumbled panic.

The hand let go of Shannon's hair and her face hit the cold floor with a slap.

Chapter 5: The Easy Way Out

Two zombies were climbing the tree. Their cold, dead hands grasped at the wet branches and pulled them up through the rain, closer and closer to the ramshackle tree house where Haws and Ash were holed up. And the closer they got, the more noise they made: snarling and shrieking. A dozen zombies now surrounded the bottom of the tree. The fireman zombie still attacked the tree with its axe. Haws looked dumbstruck.

"Zombies can climb trees?" Haws said.

Ash nodded gravely and said, "I guess zombies can climb trees."

"Shitting fuck," Haws said calmly.

"You're taking this news very well," Ash said.

They watched as the two zombies climbed slowly up the branches. When one slipped, it grabbed for a branch and in catching it, its rotting arm was ripped violently in two as the rest of it fell to the ground below. With a broken spine, the zombie writhed around on the floor and moaned, unable to move. Beside the broken-backed zombie stood the fireman zombie. It was hacking away at the tree with its axe, slowly but surely destabilizing the enormous trunk. Haws and Ash held on tight as the enormous tree began to sway.

"We're gonna have to do something about that fuckin' fireman," Haws said.

Haws pulled his shotgun out and aimed down.

"Haws, don't-"Ash began.

The shotgun blast lit up the darkness of the tree house and the fireman hit the ground. Haw laughed and said, "That takes care of that."

Ash frowned and said nothing. She waited. Then she heard precisely what she expected to hear next.

The forest came alive with the sound of the dead.

The zombies shrieked for blood. They ran as fast as they could towards the tree in which she and Haws sat.

The fireman sat up in the dirt. Its helmet was cracked, having taken the force of the shotgun blast, and its head beneath was unharmed, beyond being already dead. Its brain was intact. It screamed unintelligible obscenities through a rotten tongue.

"Fuck," Haws said.

"We don't have enough ammo to take them on," Ash said. "How many rounds you got?"

"A handful of shells is it," Haws said.

"Keep two," Ash said. "We might need them for ourselves."

The tree started to sway. The zombies at the bottom were beginning to climb it. The base of the trunk, where the fireman had cut, groaned under the weight of the twenty new bodies clambering up its sides.

"You can fucking put a sock in that shit," Haws said.

"I'm going down."

Haws handed Ash his shotgun. "Wait," Ash said,

"What the fuck are you going to use? Don't be an asshole."

Haws made two fists with his hands. "I got everything I need to take care of any motherfucker that moves," he said. "I'll be damned if I'm going to sit up here talking about killing myself like some little pussy."

Ash grabbed his arm. "Look," she said, "what the fuck are you trying to prove? You'll get yourself killed just as fast going down there as you would if you put this damn shotgun to your head. You can't take on twenty of those things by yourself."

Haws, with one leg on the next branch down, looked up at Ash. Since the start of all this, Haws was the one guy you could count on to be cracking jokes and grinning from ear to ear. Ash thought he genuinely enjoyed it all. He didn't worry her, but she was glad she wasn't his enemy. Right now, though, there was no joke and there was no smile.

"It's over," Ash said, trying to hold back the tears. "It doesn't have to hurt. There's no shame in doing it ourselves. We lasted longer than anyone else. This is a win."

Haws shook her hand off his arm and looked down at the horde of zombies. "Suicide is for fuckin' cowards," he said. "I don't give two shits how hard or how scary shit gets, that ain't an answer. Ain't no way to go out."

"It's not the same," Ash said. "Ever since this whole thing started, we've been on borrowed time."

"It's always the same," Haws said. "Giving up is giving up. I'm not going out like a bitch."

158

"You can't take them all on yourself."

"Watch me," Haws said. And his smile returned. He lowered himself down to the next branch down. A zombie was crawling slowly up between the branches, gasping and gnashing broken teeth together. Haws put a boot through its face and sent it tumbling down the tree. It hit every branch on the way down and lost limbs and chunks of flesh and bone with every impact, until it hit the floor as almost a mush of dead meat. It was a hell of a climb down, especially with the tree swaying as the fireman hacked at the trunk, but it was better than staying, Haws thought. He wasn't gonna let a bunch of deadheads finish him off in some shitty little forest in the middle of nowhere. He wasn't gonna hide in some kid's tree house until his time was up.

And, seeing him move, Ash decided she wasn't either. She broke a plank of wood from the wall and tucked it into the back of her belt. "Hold up," she said. "Let's get this shit done together."

Haws looked up. "Atta girl," he said.

The climb down was much easier than the climb up, even with the rush prompted by the bloodthirsty zombies headed in their direction. They had pulled themselves up the tree branch by painful branch after an attack on the group left everyone scattered and running for their lives. Haws nearly fell at least twice, his muscular frame not suited to the kind of nimble maneuvering required to weave through the branches. Ash had to drag him up onto the tree house.

The tree swayed and started to tip as Haws and Ash neared halfway down. The fireman was getting through.

"Don't stop," Haws said.

159

Haws kicked out at a zombie who met him on the way up. His boot smashed its lower jaw off and it kept coming. Haws kicked again at its chest and his foot went right through its ribcage, through the rotten mush which had once been internal organs and out the other side. The zombie fell off the tree, releasing the branch it was holding, and got stuck on Haws's boot, weighing him down and nearly pulling him off the tree.

"Fuck!" Haws said. "Need a hand here, Ash!"

Ash swung to the next branch down and grabbed the zombie by the arm and yanked as hard as she could. The arm ripped clear off the body and Ash felt herself begin to fall. Haws watched in horror as her Ash's slipped from under her and she slid down into the dark branches below. Her scream stopped for a moment as she became tangled, then began again as she plummeted farther down.

"Ash!" Haws shouted.

Haws shook his leg but the zombie was gripping him with its remaining hand. Haws held onto the tree with all his strength as the weight of the zombie dragged him down. He swung his leg back and forth to free himself. He felt the zombie's bones pressed against his knee. Haws pulled himself up with everything he had and looped an arm over the thick tree branch. With his other hand, he pulled the shotgun from his back and pressed it directly against the zombie's chest. A hot blast from the shotgun tore through the zombie's rib cage and smashed its spine into tiny fragments. What was left of the zombie fell away from Haws's leg. Haws checked his leg for scratches, wiping away the blood and his torn jeans, and, seeing nothing, started climbing towards where Ash fell into a dark tangle of branches.

Haws swore to himself the whole way down: "Fuckin' stupid, undead fuckin' assholes coming up into our shit and fuckin' everything up. Fuckin' get my foot stuck in his fuckin' chest."

Just below halfway down the tree he saw Ash slumped over a thick branch with blood around her head. He was halfway to her when the whole tree began to fall.

*

Haws was on a beach. He was riding a motorcycle with a drink in his hand and the wind in his face. He was doing his best to smile, but something was irritating him, some sound. He couldn't place it. He stopped the bike and threw away the drink in anger. He looked all around the bike for the source of the sound, a loud, repetitive knocking. He moved the handlebars. He looked over every square inch of the engine of his beautiful, brand new Harley. He found nothing, but the noise continued. He couldn't place the source. He thought maybe it was in his head.

Haws opened his eyes and saw the source. He was back in the wet, cold forest and a thick branch that lay on top of him, a branch bigger than most trees, was all that stood between Haws and the blade of the fireman's axe.

Haws was trapped.

He couldn't see Ash anywhere.

The blade of the axe landed in the branch in front of Haws's chest. He pushed upwards on the branch and felt movement. He couldn't throw it off, but maybe he could slide out, he thought. His muscles burned with the strain as he pushed up on the thick, heavy branch as the fireman tried to pull its axe free of the wood.

161

The branch fell back down on Haws. This is it, he thought. Some fucker in a fireman's outfit is gonna axe me in the face and I'm done. His life didn't flash before his eyes in the traditional sense. He knew it was coming now. The fall had taken it out of him. There was no moving. There was no getting out of this one. But it wasn't a series of images that flashed through his mind, not like in the movies. Haws, instead, had a series of thoughts in quick succession. He ran through the people in his life, past and present. He thought about them each for only a split second, but for each he could easily recall a good memory. The assholes, they didn't make an appearance. All that mattered were the good people: his mom, his brother, his friends from back in the day, Barcomb, Ash. He thought only good thoughts. He was pissed that he was about to die, but he was overcome with gratitude. Though he felt like he was dying like a chump, he was happy he'd lived like a fuckin' bad motherfucker. He gave the branch one last push, but he had nothing left.

"Come on then, you little prick," Haws said. "Do your worst."

The fireman stood over the branch, placing one foot on top of it and making it crush Haws's chest further. It lifted the axe above its head and hissed through a face which was making a scream. Haws thought it was almost smiling. Haws shut his eyes and thought of Hawaii. He'd always wanted to go, ever since he was a kid.

Haws's eyes were closed for what seemed like forever. And then there came a sound.

"Are you enjoying your fucking nap time there?"

Haws opened his eyes. It was Ash. She smiled. Ash had hold of the axe. The fireman was beheaded on the

162

ground beside her. Its head was still snapping and hissing. Ash took the axe to the branch and within a few minutes had cut Haws free.

"I thought I was a goner," Haws said, taking her hand to get up.

Ash laughed.

"I thought you were too," he said.

Ash wiped her own blood away from her face and said, "Not this time. It's just a bash. I'll live."

"That's a very optimistic attitude," the man behind her said, pulling the hammer back on his pistol.

Ash turned and saw a man in a suit holding a pistol in one hand and an AR-15 in the other. Behind him, just out of the way behind the trees, she could see the lights of a six-wheeler truck through the rain.

"We don't want any trouble," Ash said.

"Well," the man said, "trouble is what you have."

Ash took a step back to be beside Haws.

"What are you doing around these parts?" the driver of the truck said.

"None of your fuckin' business," Haws replied.

"Looking for shelter," Ash said. "That's all."

Ash eyed the fireman zombie's severed head on the floor. Its mouth still snarled and snapped, though it made no noise.

"Who are you?" the driver asked.

"Name's Ash, and this is Eddie."

"What's your fuckin' name?" Haws asked.

"Fuck you," the driver said. "That's my name."

"Cute," Haws said with a snarl.

"Well, I'd take you with me," the driver said, "but I got a full house already. I guess I'm just gonna have to kill you."

Ash saw something move in the shadows in the trees. It looked like a person on all fours. She jerked back from it instinctively. "What the fuck is that?" she said. She looked at Haws and looked back and whoever it was had gone.

The driver smiled. "That's just Pocahontas," he said.

"Pocahontas?" Ash said.

"Say it louder," the driver said. "You'll see. Go on." Ash was reluctant.

"Well," the driver said, "if you don't want to meet Pocahontas I might as well just kill you now."

"Pocahontas," Ash said, in the direction of the shadows. "Pocahontas."

"Louder," the driver said.

"Pocahontas," Ash said, louder.

From out of the shadows came a woman on all fours, painfully thin with knife-cut hair and big dark eyes, eyes that hadn't slept for weeks. Ash felt immediately sick upon seeing her.

"What-" Ash said. "What have you done to that woman?"

"I don't see a woman," the driver said. "What woman?"

Haws scowled at the sight of her. "You sick fuck," he said.

"Oh, this isn't my dog," the driver said. "This is my boss's dog."

"You need to find a better employer," Haws said.

"Mr. Torrento is very generous with his friends," the driver said.

"Torrento?" Ash said.

"You've heard of him?" the driver said, surprised. Ash nodded.

"What have you heard?" the driver asked. "Have other people heard?"

Pocahontas walked on bleeding hands and feet in between the driver and Haws and Ash.

"I've heard he's crazy," Ash replied. "Supposed to be some big scary drug kingpin."

165

The driver nodded, interested. He lifted his pistol and pointed it at Ash's head. "Mr. Torrento doesn't like it when people have heard of him. It means he hasn't done a good job," the driver said. "But you're too pretty to go to waste. I got a man and a woman in the truck. I'm seriously considering killing the man and taking you in his place. Mr. Torrento likes his meat, but he loves his dogs."

Ash frowned. Pocahontas sniffed at Ash's leg.

"What do you say, pretty lady?" the driver said. "You can die right here, or you can come with me. You'd make an excellent house pet. Look at that mouth. What do you say?"

Ash looked at Haws. Pocahontas growled up at Haws. Haws nodded to Ash.

"OK," Ash said. "Let him go, and I'll come with you."

The driver thought for a moment. "Nope," he said.

He raised the AR-15 and, before it came up, Ash swung a leg out as hard as she could and kicked the fireman zombie's severed head in the driver's direction. Haws rolled to the ground and picked up his shotgun. The driver got off a couple of rounds before the severed zombie head struck him in the chest and knocked him down. Haws ended his roll on one knee with his shotgun aimed at the floored driver's head. Haws didn't even think. The trigger pulled itself. The driver's face and skull and hair exploded in a thick fog.

Pocahontas leaped onto Haws's back and scratched at him. She sunk her sharpened teeth into his back and drew blood, tearing out a chunk of flesh. Haws grabbed her by the arm and twisted hard until she flipped down in front of him

166

and writhed to get free. Ash jumped in and leaped on top of Pocahontas, sitting on her bare chest and holding her arms down by the wrists. She thrashed and barked and growled and made squealing noises as Haws picked up the AR-15 and pointed it at her head.

"What the fuck is going on?" Haws said, putting his finger on the trigger.

Pocahontas's squawking and forced barking became frantic. And then a word came through. The word was "Please." She barked a dozen more times and never stopped fighting, and then that word came again: "Please."

Ash looked at Haws, concerned.

Haws raised the butt of the gun to his shoulder, ready to fire.

The word came again. It was unmistakable, even amid all the growls and thrashing: "Please."

Haws lowered his gun. Ash let go of Pocahontas's arms and they immediately retracted to wrap around and cover her own head in a protective layer. Ash stood up and Pocahontas nearly curled up into a ball like a hedgehog. Her barks and growls became howls of despair, cries of utter hopelessness.

"Please," she said.

Her crying was loud. The shotgun sound worried Ash. Zombies would be coming.

Ash knelt beside Pocahontas and put a hand on her shoulder. When she felt the hand on her, Pocahontas recoiled in terror and screamed.

"It's OK," Ash said, over and over. "We're not going to hurt you. You're safe."

Haws took off his shirt and lay it over her body, now bare-chested himself.

"We're gonna have to calm this girl down or she's gonna bring Hell down on us," Haws said. "Let's get to the truck."

Ash put her face beside Pocahontas's ear and whispered: "We're not going to hurt you. You're safe. You're with friends. Friends are here. You're safe. Let's get to the truck."

Ash lifted Pocahontas by the arm and she gingerly moved towards the truck. She was still wailing. Haws said, "Fuck this," picked her up over his shoulder and carried her to the truck, enduring the bites and scratches as she struggled to get free. Ash ran ahead and opened the door and Haws put her inside and shut it after. Inside, she seemed to quiet down.

"I guess this Torrento guy is somewhere around here," Haws said.

"And we should get the fuck out of here as soon we can," Ash said.

"Agreed," Haws said. "I don't want any part of this kind of crazy. That was a Hell of a kick you got on you there with that fuckin' head, I gotta say."

Ash shrugged. "I played a lot of soccer in high school."

168

"Saved by a fuckin' soccer player," Haws laughed. "What is the world coming to?"

A bang from the truck's storage compartment grabbed their attention. Haws frowned at Ash, then gestured to her to get ready to open the hatch. He raised the AR-15 and nodded to her.

Ash flipped it open.

"Motherfucker," Haws said with a smile.

"Motherfucker yourself," Barcomb said, grinning back from inside the compartment.

"Help us out of here," Munday added. "This shit is cramped."

Barcomb doubled over in agony when he was pulled out of the compartment. He was bleeding bad.

"Holy shit, bro," Haws said. "What the fuck happened to you?"

"Couple gunshots," Barcomb replied, glancing at Munday. "Nothing a nice lie down won't fix."

"We have to get you help," Ash said. "Right fuckin' now."

Barcomb said, "I'll be fine, so stop your fuckin' fussing." He got to his feet and then fell back down. Haws caught him on the way. The rain was washing the blood away, but more kept coming.

"If we don't get him some help," Ash said, "he won't last the night."

169

"We're fuckin' miles away from any city," Haws said.

"We don't even know where we are," Munday chimed in.

Ash rubbed her temple and thought. She could see the head of the fireman zombie in the corner of her eye. As she thought, she walked over to it, grabbed the axe and swung it down into the fireman's head, neatly dividing its skull and brain in two, the latter sliding out onto the ground. The mouth slowed and then stopped moving with a surprised look on each half of the face.

Ash turned and looked at the truck as everyone watched her.

"Pocahontas knows where we are," Ash said.

Everyone looked at her, confused.

"And there's a house nearby. Torrento lives around here, right?"

"He must," Haws pondered, "But we can't-"

Barcomb slipped again into unconsciousness.

"We have to," Ash interrupted Haws. "We find Torrento's house and we make some kind of deal. If he won't make a deal, we take the place for ourselves. And Pocahontas will show us the way."

"What if she won't?" Munday asked.

Chapter 6: The House on the Side of the Hill

Pocahontas slumped in the seat and cried.

"We don't have time for this," Ash said.

Ash, Haws and Pocahontas were crammed into the front of the truck. Haws was behind the wheel. Barcomb was unconscious on the bunk in the back while Munday sat on the edge beside him. The truck was still. Barcomb's blood was dripping down onto the floor. Everyone could feel it warming the underside of their boots. He looked pale.

"Which way?" Ash shouted.

Pocahontas pointed down the left fork, then the right fork, then the left again before breaking down into more tears.

"Come on!" Ash screamed.

"We've been out here an hour now," Munday said. "Barcomb doesn't have time." She looked at the blood pooling up around him on the bunk. Her hands were shaking. She couldn't look anyone in the eye. The scratch on her cheek still stung and she was out of patience. If this man died, she would be responsible. She eyed Haws's knife which he had placed in a holster in his belt. "Everyone get out. Leave her with me."

Ash and Haws turned and looked at her.

"I'll get her talking," Munday said. She felt tears in her eyes. She felt her voice shaking.

"No fuckin' way," Haws said.

"Are you kidding?" Ash asked.

Munday calmed. She looked at her boots.

Ash sighed.

"Sor-" Pocahontas said, drooling through her sharpened fangs. "Sorry."

Munday pulled Haws's knife and drew it to Pocahontas's neck in one motion, grabbing her hard by the hair with her other hand. Pocahontas screamed as the blade slowly separated the top layer of her skin and blood dribbled down.

"Which fuckin' way to the house?!" Munday screamed in her ear. "Which fuckin' way?!"

Pocahontas flapped her arms around and cried. Munday pressed the knife harder against her throat and drew more blood.

"What the fuck are you doing?" Ash shouted.

Haws went to punch Munday, but she shouted, "Back off!" and pressed the knife harder, making Pocahontas scream.

"This bitch is gonna tell us where this fucking house is or she's gonna lose her fuckin' head!" Munday screamed.

"L-le-left!" Pocahontas screamed. "It's left! I remember now! I remember!"

Everyone calmed. Munday held the knife to her throat. "You're wrong," she whispered in Pocahontas's ear, "and I'm gonna take off your fucking head. I promise you that."

Munday lowered the knife and looked at Haws.

"You heard her," she said. "Left."

Haws started up the engine and felt safe enough to turn the headlamps back on now that they were about to move. He rolled the truck forward.

Haws took the right turn.

"What the fuck are you doing?" Munday shouted and punched him in the back of the head.

Haws shoved her back and she landed on her ass on the bunk.

"She fuckin' said left, you dumb asshole!" Munday said.

Ash frowned, unsure, and looked at Haws as he sped down the right turn between the trees that were low enough to scrape the roof of the truck.

"Where the fuck are you taking us?!" Munday shouted.

He's gonna fuckin' die, Munday thought. , and it's all my fault. I fuckin' killed him and this son of a bitch is making damn sure he dies. What the fuck!

Haws was furious, staring straight ahead, clenching his jaw and gripping the steering wheel so hard his knuckles were white.

Munday pulled a gun on Haws. "Stop the fuckin' truck," she said. "Right now, you motherfucker!"

"Calm the fuck down!" Ash shouted.

Munday swung the gun to aim at Ash.

"Shut the fuck up!" Munday shouted.

The gun was away from Haws just long enough for him to assess the situation in the rear view mirror. He swung a well-placed elbow back as firmly as he could and Munday's nose snapped on impact. She dropped the gun and fell backwards, joining Barcomb on the bunk and in unconsciousness.

*

The truck was stopped when Munday came back around and everyone was stood outside, even Barcomb. She was alone on the bunk.

"Great," Haws said, popping his head in. "She woke up."

Ash rolled her eyes.

Munday looked around, dazed. She felt for her gun and the knife first. They weren't there, so she felt her nose. She winced in pain. Her hand was covered in blood.

"Let's get our fuckin' game faces on," Barcomb said. "Stop all this fuckin' around, right now." He leaned on the side of the truck and pointed up the hill to a house at the top. "That's the place. It's gotta be."

Pocahontas was cowering near the wheels, on her knees and shivering all over with wide eyes.

"How did you know Pocahontas was lying?" Ash asked.

Haws looked at Pocahontas and she shrank down and covered her head. "I've seen a lot of shit in my time," he said. "I took a stint in the army and saw time in Afghanistan. One of the things I saw a lot of - it got a little press later on, but the shit was everywhere - was torture. Early on, every motherfucker was at it. The only problem was - which was something they figured out pretty quick - was that when you beat someone long enough, when you threaten their family or fuckin' drown them all night, those motherfuckers would say anything to make it stop. This girl here, looking at what they done to her, that's the last fuckin' place she'd ever want to go. Some bitch puts a knife to her throat and asks for an answer, she's gonna tell her the other fuckin' way."

Munday climbed down out of the truck's cab, nursing her broken nose.

"You got an answer, but that don't necessarily mean you got the answer you wanted," Haws said. "She told you the way she wanted to go."

Munday scowled at Pocahontas. She heard a click next to her head. It was Barcomb's gun.

"You pull any shit like that while I'm awake," Barcomb said, "and you can kiss your ass goodbye. You're lucky we don't march you off into the fuckin' woods right now."

"I was trying to help," Munday said.

"Well," Barcomb replied, "don't."

175

"So, there it is," Ash said, looking up at the house.

Pocahontas crawled behind Haws's legs. He looked down at her. She had tears in her eyes. "Must be," he said.

"It looks like it'll take some work to get inside this place," Barcomb said, still half-dazed with blood loss, slurring his speech and just about standing with the help of the truck. The sun was rising behind them and the light shone on the ground wet with last night's rain. It glistened on the wet walls surrounding the house. When Barcomb saw the heads on top of the wall, he knew exactly what kind of place this was and what they'd have to do to get inside. Twelve-foot concrete walls surrounded the house, turning it into more like a compound, and the top of the wall was lined with barbed wire and periodic spikes protruding upwards. On these spikes were the heads of men and women. They were in varying stages of decomposition – some were nearly skulls – but they were all still moving. Their mouths moved in slow motion and their mournful eyes scoured their surroundings. They almost looked like they were trying to speak. Barcomb squinted to see. He watched the face of a young woman and tried to see why her mouth was moving. It seemed to be saying something. Barcomb wasn't a lip reader, but, to him, it looked like the woman's undead severed head was saying something; it was saying "Go back." It sent a chill down his spine, an icy spider that crawled up his back, cutting through the agony he was in to tell him something was very wrong with this house.

"Jesus," Barcomb said. "Dutroux made Torrento sound like the devil himself. Doesn't look like he was far from the truth. Who is this fuckin' guy?"

"How the fuck are we gonna get past this security?" Haws said. He looked at Barcomb, who he was supporting on one shoulder, and he was very pale and drifting in and out of consciousness. "How are we gonna get in?"

"We're just gonna walk up to the front gate and ask," Barcomb said. "We can't fight our way in. We have to be smart."

"Maybe it's not so bad," Ash said. "Maybe they're OK. Maybe this is just to scare people away." Ash didn't look like she believed it. Pocahontas stood on all fours beside her and trembled and wet herself.

*

The truck rolled to a stop outside the gates and the engine roared one last time before settling into a constant, low rumble. The horn sounded three times. Above the sliding wrought iron gate was a small watchtower with a shelter at the top. A long-haired, bearded man in shorts and t-shirt appeared holding an assault rifle. He looked as if he'd just stopped by to guard the house on his way back from the beach.

"Open the gate!" the watchtower guard shouted down to the man below.

The gate slid open and the truck crept slowly inside. When it stopped, the watchtower guard climbed down, smiling.

"Fuck's sake, Chuck," the guard said. "You been gone for fuckin' ever. You better have brought back some cigarettes."

The truck door opened and out stepped Eddie "The Sledgehammer" Haws. The guard stopped smiling and raised his assault rifle.

"Who the fuck are you?" the guard demanded.

Haws raised his hands. "I ain't here for a fight."

"You picked the wrong fuckin' house, cocksucker," the guard screamed.

Haws moved fast. He pushed the rifle aside with his left hand, grabbed the guard around the back of the head with his right, and thrust a knee at full speed up into the guard's nose, shattering it and knocking him out cold. Haws put his hands back up in the air as other guards ran over.

"Settle down, fellas," Haws said. "Like I said, I ain't here for a fight."

"What the fuck was that then?" another guard asked.

"That wasn't a fight," Haws said. "There's two people in a fight. And, besides, he was being an asshole. I just came to talk. Who owns this place?"

An older man walked up to Haws. He was holding a shotgun. He was black and muscular with dreadlocks, dressed in torn jeans and a dirty vest. He spoke in a thick Jamaican accent. "Nah, man," he said, shaking his head and frowning. "You don't wanna be meeting the man who owns this place. Trust."

"Maybe I can deal with you," Haws said. "Eddie Haws."

"Winston," came the reply. "What you wanting here, Eddie? You look like a dangerous man, but this is a very dangerous place. The boss man finds out what you done, you might already be in more trouble than you can walk away from."

"Well, let me fill you in on everything I've done, yeah?" Haws said. "Then we can see how much trouble I'm in."

Winston lowered his gun and listened.

"Let's start with how I just knocked out one of your guys even though he had a gun on me," Haws said. "How much trouble am I in for that? Let's talk about the truck, while we're at it. I took this truck from another one of your guys. How much trouble am I in for that? You could go talk to the guy – real sharp looking' guy in a suit – but I cut his fuckin' head off with an axe."

Three other armed men had gathered around the truck at this point. The youngest of them drew his pistol on Haws and took two steps towards him. He moved to pistol-whip Haws, but Haws dropped a shoulder, dodging it, and in half a second had snapped the kid's forearm. He fell to the ground and dropped his gun, screaming in agony.

"Oh, fuck," Haws laughed, holding up his hands again. "I am in so much trouble here, aren't I? What a fuckin' pickle."

Winston started to grin. "Man, you're fuckin' crazy," he said.

"Or," Haws said, "Maybe I'm not the one in trouble. Maybe you all are the motherfuckers in trouble. What sort of Mickey Mouse bullshit are you running here? You got the living fucking dead running around the hillside and you got these fuckin' clowns working for you? I even tamed your

179

fuckin' dog and brought it back for you, whatever the fuck that's about."

Pocahontas was cowering in the driver's foot well. Winston saw her and frowned.

"You got some fucked up shit going on up here, but ain't none of it as fucked up as how you got a bunch of fuckin' pussies guarding it. So, I'm gonna do you a favor," Haws said with a smile. "I'm gonna help you out."

"You're gonna help us out?" Winston said.

"You're getting it." Haws pointed to the truck and said, "I got me a brother in there who's hurt bad. He needs help or he's not long for this world. He's a good dude. He's a cop. He's a fuckin' professional. And you are in serious need of some professional fuckin' help. You fix him up, me and him, we'll stick around, see if we can't get this place ship shape. Shit, you can even have your truck back."

"And if we don't?" Winston said, raising his rifle.

"We leave," Haws said. "My buddy dies. I come back here in the middle of the night and cut your throat. Or you can kill me right here and these fuckin' schoolboys you got running around get you killed in a month or two. Times are hard, so you need some hard motherfuckers on your team. You fix my buddy up, you got two of the toughest bastards you're ever likely to meet."

"And what about the girl?" Winston said.

"What girl?" Haws said.

Munday and Ash listened closely. They were huddled in the darkness in the truck's storage compartment.

"The dog," Winston said.

"Keep her," Haws said. "I don't give a fuck. Whatever floats your fuckin' boat, man."

Winston nodded. He gesture to two of the guards and they went into the truck. They pulled Pocahontas out by her legs as she tried for dear life to hold onto a seat. She screamed and screamed until one of them pistol-whipped her into unconsciousness. Haws tried to hide his contempt. Winston looked at him and Haws grinned.

"Women," Haws said, laughing.

"Get his friend," Winston said to the other men. "And take this truck out back."

He put his hand on Haws's shoulder.

"Let's introduce you to the boss man," Winston said.

The truck started up and began to move. Munday and Ash prayed they wouldn't be found. Munday held her mouth. She was sweating heavily. She was trying her best not to cough.

She was coming down with some kind of illness.

The scratch on her cheek, from the zombie's tooth, felt like it was on fire.

*

Barcomb opened his eyes and saw only shapes. The shapes moved around him, towering over him and talking to one another. He could feel their hands on him, patching him up.

"He's completely out of it," a woman said.

It was a familiar haze. He'd been shot once before. It seemed like a lifetime ago now, in a different world. There was a big push against the drug cartels operating in the city of Elizabeth. While the politicians smiled for the cameras and told stories about how great this war on drugs was, Barcomb and his crew were front and center, right in the firing line. They lost seventeen cops that year. Barcomb could've been eighteen, but the bullet missed his heart by a hair's breadth. A few inches over and he'd be paralyzed for life. Barcomb knew he got lucky. A lot of other guys weren't so lucky. As the shapes and the sounds drifted in and out of a colorful haze, Barcomb expected to wake up as before, with the guys from the force gathered around his bed cracking jokes and opening beers.

Instead, there were two women.

"He looks like a cop," one voice said. "I think he's got a badge on him. Look."

"That's the last thing Torrento wants around here," the other said.

"Maybe he can help us."

"Not all cops are good guys, Gina."

"We need all the help we can get, right? What if he is a good guy? We could get out of here."

"Have you looked outside the walls recently? This is the safest gig in town."

"I can't have them touch me again."

"Look. We do what we have to."

Barcomb looked up. They weren't looking at him. They hadn't seen him wake up yet.

"All we have to do is stab that fucker in the head one day. He won't see it coming."

"His men would tear us apart."

Barcomb glanced around the dingy room, a basement set up like a medical clinic with very little real equipment. Scalpels were kept in empty milk bottles full of sterilizing agent. The bed was a fold-out camp bed placed on top of some crates. Even the partition, which wasn't drawn anyway, was a shower curtain. Barcomb saw the door and he saw that this place wasn't guarded. He didn't know if he had the strength to get up and get out of the room by himself.

"You think this guy's gonna be any help? He's half-dead. Look at him."

Barcomb shut his eyes. He pretended to sleep.

"Torrento doesn't like new people," someone said. "They'll be dead and buried soon enough. Best not to get our hopes up."

He thought maybe it was best to…

Barcomb slipped quickly back into unconsciousness.

183

Chapter 7: The Cost of Business

Torrento's house was a low-slung, three-story, modern building with flat roofs and ceiling-to-floor windows which looked out across the burning countryside, destroyed highways and desolate towns towards the dark skyline of New Jersey and New York City beyond. Inside was tastefully decorated with art and furniture from all over the world, most from Asia and the Middle East. Almost every painting or sculpture was a depiction of something violent, either a battle or a murder. The walls were primarily white and various swords were attached to them on racks dotted around the corridors. Haws could make out faint pink stains in the white, places where the blood wouldn't quite wash out. He was led through, past an indoor swimming pool, to a large dining area where Torrento was eating a large plate of roast lamb shoulder with vegetables. In the top of the lamb, the chef had stuck a little paper flag of Iraq. Torrento paid it no notice. The man leading Haws through spoke with a European accent - maybe French, Haws thought, or somewhere around there - and had a bushy ginger beard and a shaved head. Haws wasn't impressed by the guy.

"Take a seat," the Frenchman said.

"I'll stand," Haws replied.

The Frenchman tried to stare Haws down. Haws scowled.

"I've taken out half the fuckin' workforce of this house this morning already," Haws said. "If you want to get on that list, you go ahead and keep on looking at me like that."

The Frenchman looked away and tried to make a show of being proud and not caring. Haws didn't buy it. The guy is a fuckin' pussy, he thought. The Frenchman walked off. Haws watched him leave. Then he sat down.

Haws turned back to look at Torrento. Torrento was already looking at him. He'd been watching. He wiped his mouth on a napkin and stood.

"I wanted to sit down," Haws said.

"Your name," Torrento said. "What is it?"

Haws knew immediately from the way he carried himself that this was Torrento and that this was his house. Haws wasn't expecting an Iraqi. It threw him.

"I haven't got all day," Torrento said.

"Eddie Haws. You must be Mr. Torrento."

"You know of me?"

"I've heard, yeah."

"Where have you heard?"

Eddie nodded to the lamb. "You gonna eat that?"

Torrento frowned. He turned and said something in Arabic to one of his men. Within a few minutes, a second plate of lamb was brought out by a young woman and placed at the table. Torrento gestured to it. Haws started eating.

"This is good shit," Haws said.

"Eddie," Torrento said, grimacing as if the very idea of it angered him to the point of pain, "where have you heard about me?"

185

Haws was chewing a mouthful of food when he answered. "Some low-life drug-dealing piece of shit. A motherfucker named Dutroux," he said. "He told me and my buddy all about you. He told us all about this place."

Torrento's right eye twitched slightly.

"Fuck knows who else he told, the loudmouth prick."

"Where is Dutroux now?" Torrento said.

Haws kept eating. It had been a week since his last real meal.

"Do you know?" Torrento said.

"Got anything to fucking drink around here?" Haws said. "Man, I am thirstier than a duck in the desert." Haws looked confused for a moment. "Is that a real saying? Fuckin' should be," he said, and continued eating.

"There is something you should know about me, Eddie" Torrento said, through gritted teeth.

"What's that?"

Torrento pulled out the biggest and ugliest handgun Haws had ever seen. It was gold-plated with an ivory grip, some kind of modified Desert Eagle. Haws almost laughed. Torrento laid it on the table. "I am not a very patient man, Eddie," Torrento said. He went quiet for a moment and saw that Haws was studying him, trying to figure him out. "You must know that my time comes with a price. When it is wasted, there will be payment. You should know that I am not thinking about threatening you right now. I do not deal in threats. I am not thinking of a punishment to give you to make you pay for your behavior here. I have punishments in mind. I have a complex system of punishments which I can bring to mind at any point. What I'm doing right now is counting, Eddie. I'm counting how much of my time you waste so that I can take from you the correct payment when we're done."

Eddie put down his fork. "Mr. Torrento," he said, "let's cut the shit. I came here with an offer for you. I'm offering my services. Way I see it, they're sorely fuckin' needed. The gang you have working for you here?" Haws leaned in. "They're fuckin' amateurs. And in this world, amateurism will get you dead faster than a bullet."

"I asked you a question, Eddie," Torrento said calmly.

"What?"

"Where is Dutroux now?"

"Dutroux's dead," Haws said.

"Dead?"

"Yeah. My buddy put a fuckin' grenade in his mouth and shoved him off a rooftop. He ain't walking away from that."

Torrento squinted as he studied Haws, looking for something. Haws sat still, letting him look. Suddenly, Torrento laughed. He laughed so hard he slapped his hand on the table. Haws started laughing, too.

"You should've seen his fucking face," Haws said. "Bam. Painted the fucking street red, he did."

Torrento, laughing, stood up. He gestured to the door, to the Frenchman who saw Haws in who was stood waiting. He came over quickly. Before Haws could stop laughing, the other man had wrapped a garrote around his throat and tightened it, immediately cutting off his air, and grabbed his right hand and twisted it behind his back. Haws tried to fight with his left hand free. Torrento grabbed hold of it with both hands and slammed it down on the table. He used one hand to take something out of a sheathe that was hidden underneath the table, bolted to the underside.

Torrento lifted up a machete.

"You seem like a professional," Torrento said, as Haws's face began to turn blue. "I will accept your offer. You can live with the others. You will earn your place. You will be one of my best men. But I will have to disadvantage you."

Haws tried to tell him no, but he couldn't speak. He could feel his bones bending in the arm twisted behind him by the unseen man.

"As I said at the beginning of our conversation," Torrento said. "I am not one for idle threats. You wasted my time, Eddie. It was only a small amount of time, but, as this is our first meeting, I must make it very clear to you how much I value my time. The men will want revenge for what you've done today, so this will serve a dual purpose. There are lessons to be learned here, Eddie, lessons that will serve you well."

Torrento held Haws's hand firmly on the table just above the wrist.

He swung the machete down through Haws's left wrist. In one motion, Haws's left hand was freed from its wrist with a small explosion of blood and a thud as the machete was buried in the wooden table. Haws's arm flew back, released by the amputation, spraying bright red blood across the ceiling. Haws was unconscious in a matter of seconds and the man behind him released the garrote.

"Burn the stump, Boris," Torrento said. "He's no good to me dead."

Haws slumped in the chair as his blood pooled at his feet, soaking through his boots and getting his socks wet. Were he awake, he would have been furious about that.

*

When Barcomb came around, he thought the ceiling was moving. Steel pipes danced left and right and then stopped central above him. He closed his eyes for a moment and listened. He heard wheels. He opened his eyes and realized he was the one who was moving. He was being wheeled along, strapped to a bed.

"Which way?" someone whispered. "Where the fuck do we go?"

"Shut the fuck up, Munday," someone else said.

Barcomb looked up and mumbled, "What the shit is going on around here?"

The bed stopped moving. Munday and Ash came in front of him to get a look at him. Ash cringed. "You look like shit run over," she said.

Barcomb tried to sit up, but his chest was strapped down.

"Why am I tied to this fuckin' thing?" Barcomb said.

Ash looked around.

"And why are you dressed like fucking-" Barcomb began, but Ash threw a sheet over his face.

"Don't say a word," she whispered.

Barcomb heard footsteps, heavy ones, coming down the hall. The bed started moving again.

"What if he-" Munday whispered.

Ash shushed her. "Keep it together, for Christ's sake," Ash said. "If they figure out what we're doing, there's no fighting our way out of this shit."

Munday coughed.

They rolled the bed quickly. Barcomb heard the footsteps getting closer, and then there was a voice.

"Hey," a man said. "What are you girls doing down here with that?"

"Another dead one," Ash said. "Doctor said to get rid of it before it, you know, he comes back and eats everyone." She laughed nervously.

"Let me take a look at him," the man said.

"We took care of him already," Ash said. "Back of the head with a screwdriver, you know? Done it so many times I could probably kill these fuckers in my sleep."

The man walked over and stopped beside the bed. Barcomb tried to make his breathing shallow enough so as to be as unnoticeable as possible.

"Who was he?" the man asked. "One of our guys?"

"No," Ash said. "You see that truck rolled in earlier with the big dude in it?"

"I saw that, yeah," the man replied. "Big motherfucker."

"This is his friend."

"This gonna cause us a problem, you think?" the man said. "That guy was really fucking keen to save his friend. I don't want to be having that guy wandering around the place pissed off and looking for a fight, I tell you what."

Ash laughed, "No shit."

The man went quiet for a minute. Barcomb listened close.

"So, uh," the man said. "Is there any meat off this one or what?"

Ash was thrown. "Um, err," she said, "how do you mean? You want meat?"

"What kinda shape is he in?" the man said.

"Real bad," Ash said. "Hideous, actually. Yep. He's all tore up."

"I mean, it's been a while since anyone but the boss man has had any meat," the man said. "There's nothing you can save?" Barcomb felt the man's hand grab the sheet above his head. He started to pull but stopped suddenly as extra weight came down. Ash had put her hand on his arm.

"He was bit," Ash said. "Bit all over. He's tainted meat. You don't want any of what he's got, trust me."

"Maybe I better take a look anyway," the man said. "There might be a little something down there I could-" The sound of the slice of a blade on flesh stopped the man mid-sentence. Barcomb opened his eyes and the white sheet over his head was splattered with red.

"Whoa!" Ash said. "What the fuck was that?! What are you doing?!"

The man slumped on top of Barcomb. Ash pulled the sheet off Barcomb's face and he could see that the man's throat was cut and he was pouring blood all over him. Munday grabbed the man by the hair and rammed her knife through the back of his skull. Then she dropped him to the floor, his pierced skull cracking more as it hit the concrete.

"Fucking unstrap me," Barcomb said to Ash.

She undid the strap around his chest. Barcomb sat up. Munday looked at him and said, "He was gonna raise the alarm."

"This wasn't the fuckin' plan," Barcomb said.

"Yes," Munday said. "It was."

"Nobody needed to die," he said.

"It's too late for that now," Munday replied.

Barcomb glared at her. She began coughing. A little blood came up.

"What is it?" Barcomb said. "Have you been bitten?"

"No," Munday said. "It's just a cold."

Barcomb looked at Munday. She was blushing a little. He made a mental note of that.

"I know where we can hide this body," Ash said.

*

"I don't want there to be any hard feelings over this," Torrento said, dangling Haws's severed hand by its little finger in front of its previous owner. "This is a lesson. If you learn it, you will have a place here. If you refuse, there will be nowhere you can hide. This will be the last day of your life."

Haws was slumped against the wall outside the house next to a barbecue, breathing in the smell of his own cooked flesh, drooling from the shock and the pain through gritted teeth, trying real hard, and failing, to avoid looking like he wanted to kill every motherfucker in sight.

"We've burned it, so you won't bleed to death," Torrento said.

"Aren't we little angels?" Boris, the bald, bearded pussy said with a smile.

"Usually," Torrento said, "I make people eat whatever I cut off. But I can see that won't be necessary today. Will it?"

Haws took a few deep breaths and said, "No."

193

Torrento smiled. "Get him up, Boris."

"Let me give you a hand," Boris said, laughing.

Haws stood up by himself. "Get the fuck away from me, Frenchie," he said.

The pain was beginning to dull as Haws got used to it. Most people were crushed by pain. Haws, he thrived on it, turned it into anger. He let his anger bubble under the surface and he had a good look around. He was gonna feed Torrento his own balls, but not yet.

Haws saw three people moving in the shadows across the courtyard, past the parked cars. They were carrying something heavy and trying real hard not to be seen. Haws smiled. Hand or no hand, it was going to plan.

Torrento walked away, saying, "Take him to the bunk house and get him set up, Boris, then go see about his friend. See if my girls haven't sewn him up yet."

"Come on, Captain Hook," Boris said. "Let's find you a nice bed to cry in."

The bunk house was a five-car garage with beds bolted into the walls. From the number of beds, Haws guessed there must've been around twenty-five people in all.

"Where the women sleep?" Haws asked.

"Outside, usually," Boris said. "They go wherever the fuck they want. Most of the women here," Boris said with a smile, "they don't last too long."

194

Haws gritted his teeth. He could feel his fist clenching on the hand that wasn't there anymore.

Four guys rose from their bunks and two in the back playing cards stepped up. They were big guys, angry-looking guys, a little out of shape and more than a little ugly. They looked Columbian.

"Who the fuck is this punk?" one said. He looked like Dwayne Johnson if Dwayne Johnson was conceived in a car crash and raised by coyotes.

"This is Eddie Haws," Boris said. "Eddie here is gonna be joining us all. He says he's doing us all a big fucking favor, too."

Haws gritted his teeth until his jaw hurt.

"This fuckin' faggot?" another said. He looked like a Columbian late-stage John Travolta, bald head, goatee and all.

Dwayne Johnson and John Travolta got up close. The other four crowded behind them. Haws tried to the pain of his stump out of his head. He'd fought through pain before, but nothing like this. But these motherfuckers, he kept telling himself. These motherfuckers...

"Torrento got this bitch already, huh?" Dwayne Johnson said.

Haws squared up to him.

"Well, look at this puta," Dwayne Johnson said. "Looks like he ain't taken enough of a beating already."

"Go and get more men," Haws growled. "Let's make this a fair fight."

Boris almost pissed his pants laughing.

"You got a death wish, cocksucker?" John Travolta said. "Not enough you lost your hand, you want to lose your life too?"

"Make him feel at home, boys," Boris said as he left the bunk house.

Boris shut the door behind him and heard the crashing and the banging begin behind him. He shook his head and laughed at the dumb American with one hand. He headed over towards the Pit.

*

John Travolta took a right hook to the face and tumbled to the floor with a face full of blood. The others were on top of Haws in a heartbeat, kicking and shouting. Haws grabbed one by the foot, twisted him down to the ground and pulled until he heard it snap and felt the bone break skin. He screamed like a hungry baby and Haws moved on, kicking out and getting to his feet. Haws had never fought one-handed before, but he'd trained hard in hand-to-hand combat and he always liked getting his elbows involved anyway. He cracked Dwayne Johnson in the nose with a firm elbow and then brought a knee into his stomach, flooring him. One of the men grabbed a chair and threw it. Haws dropped a shoulder and moved aside and it smashed into one of the other men.

"I told you," Haws said with a grin, "you should have gone for more men."

John Travolta got to his feet and pulled a knife. He was holding his bloodied nose with tears running down his face.

"Motherfucker, please," Haws said. "You're gonna need more than that shitty little knife to get through this."

John Travolta charged him. Haws kicked downwards, meeting John Travolta's knee as he ran forward in full stride. The knee cracked and he screamed. As John Travolta fell, Haws grabbed the knife as he was on the way down, broke John Travolta's hand and twisted the knife around, sinking it into his throat as he hit the floor in one fluid motion. John Travolta's blood splashed up onto Haws's face.

Haws looked up at the other men. Two were left standing. They looked at each other in panic.

"What are you waiting for?" Haws said.

They charged at him at the same time. Haws snapped one's leg with a firm kick to the side of the knee and ducked a punch from the other. He came back up, grabbed the guy's arm and snapped it over his back with full force, sending the guy tumbling over him with his arm fractured in three places.

Everyone who wasn't unconscious was screaming.

Haws looked for a gun. He found one in a foot locker under a bed, a pistol. He checked the ammo, and then grabbed a pillow off the top of the bed. He walked up to each man, placed the pillow over their heads and pressed the gun into the pillow before firing, killing them instantly and muffling the sound somewhat.

The last one left was Dwayne Johnson.

"Please," Dwayne Johnson said. "Please, wait. I didn't mean it, really. You seem like a good guy. I'm sorry. I'm so fucking sorry."

Haws smothered him with the pillow and splattered his brains on the concrete floor.

"Punk," Haws said.

Haws looked for more guns.

He saw a meat hook on the wall and scowled.

Captain fucking Hook, he thought. I'll show these motherfuckers Captain Hook.

He grabbed it, took off his belt and tightened the hook onto his stump.

He laughed at himself.

"Why the fuck not?" he said.

Chapter 8: The Kennels

The man who threw Pocahontas back in the kennels, she didn't know his name, but he was the kennel master. She was sure of that. He was obese, wet with a thin layer of sweat, and dressed in a leather apron over a boiler suit with steel-capped boots. He stripped the clothes from Pocahontas with a knife and shoved her to the floor of her dark, damp cage in the small enclosure around the back of the house.

"Nice to have you back, princess," master said.

He kicked her in the stomach and she curled up into a ball and whined in pain. She ached all over. She could still feel the sting of the cut on her neck where Munday had threatened to open her up. She shivered in the lashing rain and the biting wind through her cage which, like the others, was exposed to the grim weather. The kennel master slammed the door shut and locked it.

"No food for you tonight," master said. "Bad doggy. You're supposed to be an attack dog. Instead, what do you do? You get your owner killed. Bad dog!" The kennel master spat on her through the cage and walked away.

Pocahontas was in a blind panic. She had thought she was free. She had thought that it was all over. When her owner was killed, she didn't understand right away. When she came to understand, she was deliriously happy. Her life, for the past six months, had been nothing but a series of violent acts inflicted upon her. She had come from Ireland, brought over by an American man who said she had promise as a model. He'd taken photographs and sent them to all the top modeling agencies. They were all in a bidding war. Tom Cruise had even seen her photo and expressed an interest in meeting her. That's what she was told. The reality was first pornographic videos, just to make the right friends, and then captivity and torture when one of those friends, Mr. Torrento, really took a shine to her. She remembered every kick, every punch, every cut, every broken bone, every moment of every day and night she was forced to go without food, and every assault. They filed down one tooth every day until she had the fangs they wanted. Each tooth took hours. She had never experienced pain like it and could imagine no pain worse.

This house was a living nightmare to Pocahontas, who was so badly damaged she couldn't even remember her real name. And now she was back again.

She could hear zombies outside the walls, hammering on the back gates. The truck had drawn them. It sounded like hundreds. There was no living outside, for Pocahontas, and she couldn't bear to live inside.

Her life was over, in her mind. She was so afraid she couldn't string actual thoughts together very well, but the overriding feeling was one of finality, of doom. Being back meant, for her, that she could never leave. It re-affirmed everything she'd been told since she arrived at the house: she was their property, and she always would be.

Pocahontas had fought for the first two weeks of torture. She had done everything in her power to stay sane, to try to recover in the brief breaks between the pain. She tried to focus on the absence of pain, rather than the pain. These moments were few and far between, but they gave her hope. What would it be like, she used to think, to live a whole day without pain like this? Pocahontas's fight had left her, as everyone's does after such enduring such violence. She first went through a phase of complete withdrawal. She didn't eat. She didn't sleep. She didn't look at anyone. Her eyes were closed most of the day. This last for two months. The torture continued in this time. Next came the final stage, the masters' end goal, the stage of utter fear, of complete obedience. And this became her existence for the next three or so months. She had done everything she had been asked, however horrific. She had never once even looked at one of her masters in an unpleasant way, never mind struck out at one.

She understood that this would be her only weapon, this prior obedience. They saw her as weak, dumb, a stupid animal.

That would be her way out.

She was curled in a ball in the corner of the cage, looking defeated, but Pocahontas was pressing her tongue against the tip of each of her fangs, remembering how sharp they were, remembering how much damage they could do and how much damage they had done before. She didn't know how many people she had killed for the masters, but it was too many.

There was a hunger in her belly now. It was a hunger only for destruction, her own and theirs. She knew she would die. She couldn't fight her way out of the house by herself. However, if she could make a dent in the house, if she could take with her some of those people who had taken everything away from her, she would feel a little less afraid before she died. And, she thought, that's the best she could hope for.

Pocahontas saw the gate. It was beginning to buckle under the pressure of the hundreds of zombies outside.

Pocahontas looked around at the other cages. A young man was the only other dog left. Torrento's men went through the dogs quickly as most died under the strain of torture. The men lasted longer than the women because they attracted less interest from the soldiers. Pocahontas tried to get the other dog's attention. He was cowering. Pocahontas did something incredibly risky to get him to look at her. She stood up. It took considerable effort to do it – she'd been beaten half to death every time she was caught walking only on her legs – but it felt right. She was filled with panic, being exposed like that, but she knew it was how she was meant to be. She almost remembered.

The other dog must've been quite new. He still had his words. "Sit down," he whispered. "What the fuck are you doing?!"

She looked for words to answer. "Kill," she said. She was surprised by the sound of her own voice. It was gentler than she imagined it to be. She hadn't been allowed to use words for months either and her memories of using them had been almost totally overwritten by memories of pain.

Pocahontas walked to the door of her cage and said it again louder.

"Kill," she said.

The other dog tried to shush her. "You'll piss them off. Please, stop! I can't take it anymore. Please, don't bring them back!"

Pocahontas shouted, "Kill!" She rattled her cage and screamed, "Kill!"

A flashlight appeared near the wall at the foot of the garden and a guard ran over. Pocahontas remembered his face. He had visited her a lot.

"What's got your panties in a bunch?" he said.

Pocahontas looked at him. She was terrified. She mumbled, "Kill."

"What are you doing on two legs?" he demanded. He holstered his gun and rolled up his sleeves. He took a key off his belt and unlocked the cage. Stepping inside, he said "Two legs bad, Pocahontas!"

He hadn't holstered his gun right.

He hadn't banked on Pocahontas knowing how to use it.

He swung for Pocahontas and she ducked, grabbed the pistol from the guard's belt and fired into his crotch. He hit the floor screaming.

Pocahontas nearly dropped the gun. She remembered how she'd seen the other men hold it and she copied her memory. She crouched down and walked out of the cage. The man tried to grab her, so she fired the gun into his head and he stopped.

The other dog shouted. "Wait!" he said. "Let me out!"

Pocahontas walked over to him.

"Please," he said. "My name's Duke. Just let me out. I'm a good guy, I swear. Don't let them torture me anymore. I can't take it."

Pocahontas thought about it.

"Please," he said. "My name's Duke McBride. What's your name?"
Pocahontas shot him through the throat and walked away, leaving him bleeding to death, naked and cold in his cage. "Kill," Pocahontas said.

Pocahontas walked over to the giant, sliding steel gate.

"Two legs bad," she said to herself, showing her fangs in a wide grin.

She climbed up onto the wall and opened the gate.

The yard was suddenly swarmed with zombies, all headed for the house as the sun came up over the hills around it.

Pocahontas was feeling less afraid already.

*

"What the fuck was that?" Munday said.

"Gunfire, from the other side of the house," Barcomb said.

Ash and Munday were stood above the pit with the dead guard's bleeding corpse in their arms. Barcomb had his gun drawn, keeping watch.

"What is this fucking place?" Barcomb said, looking down at the pit.

"We passed it on the way to find you," Ash said, "after we got out of the truck. We heard one of them call it The Pit."

The Pit was a hole in the ground about six feet deep and twenty feet wide. It was a mass grave, but the bodies were standing upright and kept away from one another with leashes tied to spikes in the ground. They were muzzled with pieces of wood which had been tied around the backs of their heads with old string. The wood in their mouths was wet with spit and blood and pus and rotten lips. They all leaned into their leashes which were attached to the back of the wooden gags.

Barcomb noticed one of them, a woman with broken glasses in a once-flowery, now-shit-covered dress, was clawing at the wooden gag with its hands.

"Why are they keeping zombies here?" Barcomb said. "What's the fuckin' point?"

"I didn't notice the fuckin' gags," Ash said. "I thought they could eat this guy."

"Fuck it," Barcomb said. "Throw him in. He'll blend in. Judging by the sounds of gunfire coming from over there, it doesn't look like we'll have to worry much about going quiet."

They threw the body in and it landed with a thud. The zombies around it immediately started reaching for it. They got down, pulling at their leashes, and started tearing it apart with their bony fingers, dragging the flesh off in wet strips. They shoved it to their mouths but couldn't eat. But that didn't stop them destroying the body. In their frenzy, they reminded Barcomb of pigs. They ripped through flesh and muscle like it was nothing.

"Someone's coming," Munday said.

"Quick," Barcomb said. "Get in."

"Get in?" Ash said.

"Now," Barcomb whispered.

205

The three of them ducked down and swung their legs over the side of the pit. They stood inside and pressed themselves against the wall. The nearest zombies reacted immediately and pulled on their leashes to get to them. Their claw-like, skeletal fingers were inches away from Barcomb, Ash and Munday. Ash faced them with her back to the dirt wall. Barcomb turned around. He grabbed her hand and squeezed it. She looked at him. He made a shushing motion. The morning light cast shadows into the Pit as two men stood at the edge and looked inside.

The first man was French. "Who do we want, doctor? We'll pick you out a pretty one."

"It's enough that I have to put up with your childish perversions. Don't ask me to take part."

"It's the end of the world, doc. We all gotta get a little something."

"Well, you stay up here and indulge in your necrophilia. While you're porking dead women, I'll be in the basement saving the world."

"You really think there's a cure?"

Then there was silence.

"You better not be holding out on us," the Frenchman said. "You said there was a fuckin' cure, doc."

"There might be," the doctor said. "Not a cure, exactly, but some kind of vaccine. These people are dead. You can't cure someone of being dead. But maybe we can interrupt the process if we find out what triggers it."

"Let me fish one of these geeks out for you, then, so you can carry on saving the world."

A hand reached down into the Pit, trying to grab the leash of the nearest zombie to the side.

Oh, fuck, Barcomb thought. He's gonna let it loose.

The hand was close to the leash.

Gunshots sounded from the house. The hand stopped, mid-reach.

"What the fuck?" the Frenchman said.

Barcomb grabbed the hand and pulled. The Frenchman yelled out as he fell head first between the zombies. He turned over and looked back and saw Barcomb. He went for his gun, but a zombie grabbed his hand and started scratching through his shirt, tearing his skin open. Barcomb lifted the AR-15 and with one well-placed shot knocked the wood from the zombie's mouth. Its teeth didn't hesitate in clamping down on the Frenchman's screaming face. Its jaws locked on the Frenchman's cheek and he squealed in agony as the zombie tore a hole in his face. The others clawed at him until they made holes in his stomach large enough to pull his intestines through.

Barcomb pulled himself out of the Pit. He trained a gun on a scared-looking doctor and said, "Help me get them out!"

They both pulled Ash and Munday out. The Frenchman screamed and screamed until the zombies tore out his lungs. After that, his face still screamed but he made no sound. The noise and the thrashing of the Frenchman drove the zombies into a mania. They screeched and pulled at

207

their leashes. The spikes were beginning to come out of the ground. They saw the wooden gag come out of the other zombie's mouth and they were starting to all scratch at their own wooden gags.

Fuck me, Barcomb thought. They're learning how to get out.

Then Barcomb saw a horde of zombies numbering in the hundreds coming around the side of the house.

Oh, fuck, he thought. Someone must've opened the gate.

"Inside!" Barcomb shouted at everyone. "Now!"

Running for a sliding glass door, Barcomb heard a shot whizz by his head. He looked up to a higher floor balcony and saw a guard firing. Beyond that, he saw the roof.

Barcomb saw a helicopter.

Forget the fuckin' chopper for now, he said to himself.

Barcomb raised his rifle, fired two rounds, both landing chest shots with a spray of red mist. The guard span and tumbled over the railing and landed on the ground beside them as they entered the house. They shut the glass door and saw as the zombies devoured the dead guard on the floor.

Barcomb grabbed Ash by the arm and pulled her behind breakfast counter as they found themselves in a kitchen. Munday dived down too as plates exploded on top of the counter and the sound of gunfire echoed through the house.

Barcomb glanced in a mirror on the wall and saw three armed guards adopt positions on the other side of the kitchen behind the appliances. The zombies at the door hammered on the glass. It was beginning to crack. The guards fired again, one shot puncturing the glass, weakening it.

"Show your face, motherfucker!" one of the guards shouted.

Barcomb popped up and fired a handful of rounds into the wall behind the guards. Plaster and brick clouds burst into the air.

"I guess the quiet approach is out the window," Ash said.

Barcomb nodded. He took a moment and winced from the pain in his chest.

"Are you OK?" Ash asked her.

"I'm peachy," Barcomb said.

He leaned over and kissed her.

Ash looked surprised.

Barcomb span around and popped up above the counter and sank three bullets into the neck and head of the first guard to pop his head out. Half of the guard's head disintegrated and he felt to the floor convulsing. Barcomb jumped back down. He looked at Ash. She still looked surprised.

"Sorry," Barcomb said with a shrug.

Munday fired blind over the counter with her pistol. She looked at a huge crack developing in the sliding glass door as the rabid zombies punched and kicked at it. "We gotta get out of here," she said.

She sat back down with her back to the counter and tried to catch her breath. It evaded her. She gasped a few times and coughed, producing blood. She swallowed it down. She looked at Barcomb. He was staring right at her. He frowned. He blind-fired the AR-15 and said, "Stay here."

Barcomb jumped onto the counter and the wall behind him popped with bullets as the two other guards fired at him. Barcomb leaped forwards off the counter towards the floor as bullets sped past his head. He fired a mid-air sweeping burst of bullets towards the two guards and the other side of the room exploded in a haze of white plaster and red mist. As Barcomb hit the floor, turning to break his fall, the two guards had hit the floor with a half-dozen new holes in their chests and heads.

"Fuck!" Barcomb said as he hit the floor, the stitches straining in his chest with a shooting pain.

Ash and Munday came around and helped him up.

"We have to-" Barcomb said, before Ash interrupted him with a passionate kiss.

"That was a really stupid thing to do," she said.

"Kissing you?" Barcomb said.

"No, dumbass," Ash laughed. "You can't just run out like that. We nearly lost you once already."

"Killed them, didn't I?" Barcomb shrugged. He smiled and nodded. "Let's find Eddie and do this."

They ran for the door opposite leading into a long hallway. Munday trailed behind, holding her stomach in agony. They got into the hallway. They stopped when they saw who was at the end of it.

Pocahontas walked into view holding a man by the hair. He wore a long leather apron and boots. Pocahontas was naked with a collar around her neck and she was dripping in blood. She pushed the man she was holding back against the wall, jammed a pistol into his mouth and sprayed his brains up the wall. She let go of his hair and he dropped to the floor. She hadn't seen Barcomb, Ash and Munday yet. She kneeled down over the body and pressed the barrel of her weapon into the man's crotch. She fired three times into his lifeless corpse, destroying his genitals.

Pocahontas looked up. She looked down the corridor. She saw Barcomb, Ash and Munday looking right at her.

"Pocahontas?" Ash said.

Pocahontas raised her pistol and pulled the trigger.

211

Chapter 9: Hostage

"If you come back in here without someone's severed head in your hands, you better be ready to meet your God!" Torrento shouted at his men. "And bring me that fuckin' pilot, right now!"

Winston ducked his head and ran out with the other men as Torrento fired into the wall around them. He shut the door behind them, locking himself in his study. Torrento put his gold-plated pistol down on the desk next to a small hill of cocaine. The woman tied up in the corner of the study was crying uncontrollably. Her hands and legs were bound together and she was gagged with a piece of old cloth. Torrento went over to her and dragged her by the rope around her hands and legs to the desk, her naked body scraping across the tiled flooring. She cried out in pain, but Torrento paid no notice. He pulled her up by her hair and bundled her on top of the desk where she lay on her side facing the door. Torrento went around the desk and ducked down behind her to see if it'd work.

He decided it would.

The woman was crying and squirming, so he grabbed his pistol and shot her in the head to make her stay still. Blood landed on his cocaine pile. Angry, Torrento called her a bitch and shot her again, demolishing the top half of her skull. He put down the pistol and opened the bottom drawer of his desk. He took out two Uzis and sat in his chair behind the dead woman and listened to the gunfire outside.

Frank Gulley was lying under a bed in one of the many empty guest rooms when Winston found him.

"No!" he screamed. "I'm not moving!"

Winston fired a round into the bed and the bullet tore through, hitting the floor next to Gulley's head. "If you can't fly that chopper," Winston said, "you ain't no good to anyone, boy. I should just pop you now."

A pair of hands shot out from under the bed. "Wait!" he shouted. "I'll get out."

Gulley was 60 years old with long gray hair and gray stubble on his overweight face. He was an ex-hippy in army gear from the days of his Vietnam protests.

"Look, brother," he said, "let's me and you go. Don't take me to Torrento, please. I'm begging you, brother. That man, I've seen him do shit you wouldn't believe. Last time I took him somewhere, he threw someone out of the fuckin' chopper. And that was before all these zombies showed up. Please don't make me go."

"What the fuck you say?" Winston said. "You trying to get me killed?"

"He doesn't have to know," Gulley said. "We can just leave."

Winston punched him in the mouth. "Ain't no hiding from Mr. Torrento."

Winston stopped and turned when he heard screams and gunfire coming down the corridor. A female guard burst into the bedroom and slammed the door behind her, bracing her back against it.

"What the fuck is going on?" Winston said.

"It's that fuckin' guy!" she shouted. "He's out there! We never should've let him in!"

Her head exploded outwards as a bullet flew through the door behind her and straight through her forehead. The door shattered inwards under the force of a kick. Before Winston could move, Haws had his hand around his throat and was lifting him into the air. Winston tried to speak, to beg, but Haws walked him over to the window. Winston dropped his gun and looked over his shoulder out the window. The yard was filled with zombies tearing apart guards and each other.

"Wait," Winston said, choking. "Wait."

Haws put him down and held his new meat hook hand up to Winston's face.

"There's a helicopter," Winston said.

"Where?" Haws growled.

"On the roof, here! We have to go through Torrento's office. This guy is the pilot," he said, pointing at Gulley as he crept towards the door.

Haws aimed his gun at him. "Don't you fuckin' move," he said.

"We were gonna go," Gulley said, "but you can come with us!"

"This place is fucked," Winston said. "We gotta get goin', man."

"You're right," Haws said. "This place is fucked."

Haws jammed his meat hook into Winston's stomach and tore it upwards. His intestines hit the floor in a series of

214

splashing sounds. Haws took the hook out and kicked Winston in the chest. He flew backwards through the plate glass window and into the yard full of zombies below.

Haws turned and shot Gully in the knee as he tried to run.

"You're not going anywhere," Haws said. He grabbed the pilot by the throat and said, "Tell me about this fuckin' helicopter."

*

Pocahontas's gun was empty. Barcomb trained his AR-15 on her and walked quickly towards her.

"We're on your fucking side!" he shouted.

Ash and Munday barricaded the hallway door with a heavy grandfather clock and a table. Pocahontas leaped at Barcomb and he kicked her back down to the ground.

"What the fuck are you doing?" Barcomb asked.

She looked up at him from off the floor. "Kill," she said.

Barcomb kneeled down in front of her, putting his AR-15 on his back. "Look at me," he said. "Look at me. You don't kill us. We're your friends. We're getting out of here, you hear me? And we're taking you with us."

Pocahontas calmed.

"We need to fuckin' go," Munday said.

Pocahontas saw her and screamed in fury. She stood up and lunged for her. Munday shot her in the chest and she flew backwards, going limp on the floor.

"No!" Barcomb shouted. He punched Munday in the face and took her gun.

Ash rushed to Pocahontas and applied pressure to the small hole in her chest. "We need to get out of this hallway," Ash said.

Barcomb helped Ash drag Pocahontas into the room at the end. It was a bedroom, a child's room full of stuffed bears. They lay Pocahontas on the bed. Barcomb tore up a nearby unicorn-decorated t-shirt and wrapped it around Pocahontas's chest.

"We can't stay here," Barcomb said. He looked around. "There's a bathroom. Let's lock her in there for now."

Munday opened the bathroom door and started shouting. "Get the fuck out of there!"

Barcomb drew his rifle and turned. A middle-aged woman came out holding a pistol in the air and a 15-year-old girl cowered behind her. Munday had her gun on them both. The older woman had pitch black hair down her back and was attractive for her age, tanned and well-kept. Barcomb hadn't seen anyone so clean since this whole thing started. He'd almost forgotten what human beings looked like when they weren't covered in shit and blood.

"Who are you?" Munday demanded.

"Torrento," the girl squeaked.

"What?" Barcomb said.

"We're his family," the middle-aged woman said. "I'm Mrs. Torrento. This is my daughter, Ava."

Ash lay Pocahontas in the bathtub. She came out and took Mrs. Torrento's gun and tucked it into her torn jeans.

"We could use them," Munday suggested.

"Wait a fuckin'-" Ash said.

"Listen to me, Barcomb," Munday said. "We just stumbled across the biggest bargaining chip you could ever ask for."

"Where's your husband?" Barcomb asked Mrs. Torrento. She looked scared.

"He'll be in his study," she said. "It's on the top floor, on the balcony overlooking the main living room. He'll- He'll have…"

"What?" Barcomb said.

"Guns," she said. "He keeps all sorts of guns in there."

"Are you going to hurt my dad?" Ava asked, holding onto her mom tight.

Barcomb didn't say anything.

"Please," Ava said.

"Look, kid," Barcomb started "we-"

"Please kill him," Ava said.

Barcomb frowned. He looked at Mrs. Torrento. Her eyes were wide. Tears were streaming down her face. She nodded and said, "Please. Help us."

"Do you think he'll let us in if we take you?" Barcomb said.

Mrs. Torrento nodded. "He loves us," she said. "He would never let anyone else hurt us. We belong to him."

"Ash," Barcomb said, "put something in front of that bathroom door. Munday, you fuckin' behave yourself. I'm doing all I can right now not to shoot you in the fuckin' head."

Munday coughed up blood.

"You don't look too good," Barcomb said.

She collapsed on the floor and immediately tried to right herself and push herself back up.

"Munday, what's the matter with you?" Barcomb said. She pushed herself up again and got to her feet.

Barcomb grabbed her by the arm, hard.

"Rachel," he said. "Look at me."

Munday looked at him.

"Are you bit?" Barcomb asked.

"We need to go," Munday said.

218

"Mrs. Torrento stays," Barcomb said. "Bring the kid."

Suddenly there was a crash and the door caved inwards. A headless zombie landed on the floor. Barcomb raised his rifle and stopped just as he was about to pull the trigger.

Haws stood in the doorway with his meat hook on his stump with a zombie's severed head hanging from it, the hook through its eye.

"Barcomb?" Haws said.

"What the fuck happened to your hand, bro?" Barcomb asked.

A zombie jumped onto Haws and he held it back with the hook and shot its head clean off, the bullet smashing the skull like a raw egg.

"Maybe we should walk and talk," Barcomb said, coming out of the bedroom and seeing the hallway door caving under the pressure of the zombies beyond.

*

"This is the helicopter pilot," Haws said, dragging him down the hall.

"You can fly that thing on the roof?" Barcomb asked. "It works?"

"It works," Gulley said, nodding.

They reached the main living area. They were on the third floor and the hallway gave way to a balcony which ran around the living area two floors down. At the north of the

219

balcony, a few steps led up to a door in the center: Torrento's room. Zombies were screaming and tearing each other apart in the room below. Barcomb put his back to the wall next to Torrento's door. He held his AR-15 in one hand and Torrento's daughter, Ava, in the other. She was terrified, crying uncontrollably, shaking in her pajamas.

"Please get me out of here," she begged.

"We just need you to get inside," Barcomb said. "No-one's gonna hurt you."

Barcomb gestured to Haws and he moved to the other side of the door. The pilot was behind him. "You fuckin' stay put," Haws said.

"I want out of here as much as you," he said.

Munday and Ash brought up the rear. Ash capped a zombie who wandered onto the balcony and watched as it tumbled to the living room below leaving a trail of splatter in the air.

"Torrento!" Barcomb shouted.

The door exploded outwards under the force of a shotgun blast.

"We have your daughter!" Barcomb shouted.

"What the fuck do you people want?!" Torrento shouted. "I had it all here! I had my drugs and my guns and my soldiers and my slaves! Is that it?! Is it the fuckin' dog slaves you don't like so much? You fuckin' faggots!"

The door exploded again, producing another hole.

"Hey, Torrento!" Haws shouted. "You took my hand, you motherfucker. I'll have no problem taking your fuckin' family. We got your fuckin' wife locked up, too. You let us in, no-one has to die."

"We want the helicopter," Barcomb said. "If you want the house, you can fuckin' keep it if you can hold it."

It went silent for a moment. Then, Torrento shouted, "Alright!"

Barcomb looked at Haws, confused.

"You can come in, whoever the fuck you are!" Torrento shouted. "Just you, and just my daughter!"

Barcomb grabbed Ava around the neck and put his AR-15 on his back, drawing a pistol and putting it to her head.

"Anything goes down, Eddie," Barcomb said, "You take care of Ash, you hear?"

Barcomb looked back at Ash who was popping zombies as they came onto the balcony. She nodded at him. Barcomb went inside.

*

The first thing Barcomb noticed was the dead girl on the desk. The office was in total disarray. Weapons and ammo lay strewn around the room: Uzis, shotguns, even a rocket launcher.

"Why don't you take a fuckin' seat and tell me how this is gonna work?" Torrento said.

"I'll stand," Barcomb replied.

"Daddy!" Ava said. She tried to run to him but Barcomb held her tight. The pressure against his chest was sending shooting pain through his chest, making him woozy.

"Don't worry, sweetheart," Torrento said. "It'll all be over soon."

"What the fuck have you built here, you sick fuck?" Barcomb said.

"I am a king," Torrento said, "and this is my castle."

"How come I never heard of you? I worked Elizabeth P.D."

"Either you're very bad at your job, or I am very good at mine. I make it my business to stay invisible. I have people who do the dirty work for me. I don't even have to ask sometimes. I…"

Torrento laughed.

"I recognize you now!" he said. "Darren Barcomb!"

"You know me, motherfucker?"

"I saw you in the paper," Torrento said. "One of my associates, a low-life piece of shit named Dutroux - I believe you're familiar with him - killed your partner and sent his head by Fed Ex to the police station."

"I put Dutroux down for that myself."

"You know why he did that?"

222

"He told me he wanted to impress you, right before I kicked him off the side of a building."

Torrento grinned. "I wasn't impressed by him and I'm not impressed by you. I believe in a broader, more firm approach. I don't deal in people. I deal in families."

"Lucky for you," Barcomb said, "I don't. So you just let us through, we'll take the chopper and be out of your hair."

"You've destroyed everything I created here," Torrento said. "And you want me to just let you walk away?"

"That's right."

"Everything in this world comes with a price, Officer Barcomb. I've made mistakes and this is the price I have paid."

"You still have your family."

"Family is everything to me," Torrento said, nodding. "Let her come to me - come to me, Ava - and I'll let you through."

Barcomb ducked down behind a marble statue and raised his AR-15 as he let Ava walk across the room and around the desk to her father.

Torrento hugged Ava tight. He looked over her shoulder to Barcomb. "There's no more to be said," Torrento said. "I have my daughter... my blood."

Torrento pulled a knife from his belt and span Ava around to face Barcomb.

"Look at what you've done to me!" Torrento screamed.

He held Ava hard by the hair, pulling her head back. "Daddy, please!" she screamed.

Torrento jammed the knife into her exposed neck.

"No!" Barcomb shouted.

Ava's eyes rolled into the back of her head and she convulsed violently. Torrento twisted the knife and opened her throat up, sending her blood spilling all over the floor.

"You did this!" Torrento screamed at Barcomb, completely unhinged, his face red and his eyes wide. "You fuckin' did this to me!"

He stabbed Ava in the throat again, nearly decapitating her.

Barcomb fired, full auto, into Torrento's body, shredding his chest and disintegrating the top of his head. His brains hit the wall. He and his daughter hit the floor.

Haws, Ash and Munday rushed inside. Gulley followed sheepishly.

"Motherfucker," Haws said. He fired a shot into Torrento's corpse.

"Son of a bitch," Ash said, looking at the twitching corpse of Torrento's daughter.

"Oh, God!" they heard from the doorway. It was Mrs. Torrento. She backed up away from the scene. She started screaming at the top of her lungs.

"Wait!" Barcomb shouted.

She turned and jumped off the balcony, hitting the tiles two floors down with a crunch. She screamed, not quite dead, and was alive when the zombies set upon her and started tearing her apart.

Ash went to the window and looked out at the world. The sun had come up completely. It almost looked normal beyond the walls. Within them, zombies swarmed. The gates were still open. "What are we gonna do, Darren?" she said.

"We have to leave," Barcomb answered.

Barcomb turned and saw Munday, barely standing and with blood dripping from her mouth. She raised her Glock and fired. Ash was thrown back through the window and disappeared below its frame before she could even begin screaming. When she hit the ground outside, then she started screaming.

"No!" Barcomb shouted. He instinctively ran to the window and looked down. Ash was sprawled out below, bleeding from her stomach. She writhed in agony and screamed.

Barcomb drew his gun and turned to face Munday. Haws drew on her too.

"What the fuck do you think you're doing?!" Barcomb shouted.

Munday had her arm around Gulley's throat, choking him while she held the barrel of her Glock to the side of his head. "I'm taking the fucking helicopter," she said.

"You fuckin' crazy bitch," Haws shouted, "what's wrong with you?!"

Haws ran out of the room and started firing at the zombie. "I'll get Ash!" he shouted.

"Munday," Barcomb said, his aim wavering as he fought through the pain, "you're fucking us. What the fuck is the matter with you? We'll be fuckin' fine! We can all go together!"

"We won't be fine!" she screamed. "Have you looked out that window? Have you seen what's going on out there? We're all fucked, all of us! The only thing left to do is run. Maybe it's better somewhere else."

"It's not better," Barcomb said. "Everywhere else is just as dead as here. You heard the reports yourself. This shit is world-fuckin'-wide! Where are you gonna fuckin' go?"

"An island," she said.

"A fuckin' island? How much fuckin' fuel do you think this helicopter has?"

"Look," Gulley said, raising his hands, "that fuckin' thing's got fuel for days, but it's old as shit. I can fly it, but if that thing breaks then I can't repair a fuckin' thing. If that thing dies in mid-air, we die in a big fuckin' fireball when it hits the ground, because there's not a goddamn thing I'll be able to do about it."

"It's a risk I have to take," Munday said. Munday started dragging Gulley back towards the rear door which led to the roof, stepping around the bodies. Barcomb fired into the wall behind her head.

"If I have to," he said, "I'll fuckin' kill both of you just to stop you fuckin' us over. Look, you're sick, Munday. You fuckin' need people or you won't make it. You can't fuckin' make it on your own. I swear to God, I'll kill you both!"

"No," Munday said. "You won't."

Barcomb took two steps forward to follow them. Munday was hidden behind Gulley, ducking down slightly.

"You're too fuckin' soft, Barcomb," Munday said. "You won't make it, I can tell you that."

"I'm soft?" Barcomb said. "How the fuck do you figure that?"

"You won't do what's necessary. You won't kill an innocent person to save yourself, to save the group. You're dangerous, because you don't take the matter of survival seriously enough. The world isn't the same. We're not cops any more. There is no fucking law."

"There's law if we want it. We can't just decide to throw everything away and live like animals."

"If we don't, the animals will be the only ones left!" Munday walked backwards through the door, muttering to Gulley, "If you put a single fuckin' foot out of place I'm going to blow your fat fuckin' head off."

Barcomb growled and shook his head, aiming his gun at Gulley who was placed much too much in the way.

"Munday, don't you fuckin' do this. You walk out that door – I'm telling you – there's no coming back from that. I will put you down."

Munday shifted to the side of Gulley and fired. A bullet whizzed by Barcomb's head and he dived for cover behind a bookcase. Munday fired two more times and paper exploded around Barcomb's head as he waited for his moment. Munday's third shot was dry: she was out of ammo. Barcomb ran out from cover and saw her heading out the exit, onto a steel staircase outside the building, dragging Gulley along with him still placed in the way.

"Motherfucker, stop right there!" Barcomb barked.

Munday kept going.

Barcomb lifted his weapon and fired. Gulley's kneecap exploded in a fine red mist and he dropped instantly to the floor with a deafening scream. Munday pulled him up and he started to drop again.

"Fuck you!" she screamed, and pushed him over the railing and down to the ground below with a sickening crunch. She stopped and turned and looked right at Barcomb. Barcomb aimed at her face and pulled the trigger.

Barcomb was out of ammo, too.

"Son of a bitch," Barcomb said.

Munday turned and ran up the steel staircase.

Barcomb couldn't hear Ash screaming outside any more. He followed Munday out the door and up the stairs to the rooftop.

The sun blinded him as he climbed the stairs. His chest was bleeding, he could feel it. He felt the stitches had

228

come loose. When he reached the top he saw Munday stood on the edge of the rooftop, just beyond the helicopter.

"Where the fuck are you gonna go now?" Barcomb inquired.

Munday turned around. She was in tears. She was bleeding from her mouth and sweating and sickly. She could hardly stand.

"Who the fuck do you think you are?" Barcomb asked.

"I'm Rachel," Munday said. "I've put up with people like you all my life and tried to make something of myself and this is where it gets me."

"People like me?" Barcomb shouted. "I've saved your fuckin' life!"

Barcomb could hear the zombies coming through Torrento's office now, banging and barging their way through in a violent rage.

"Some fuckin' life you saved!" Munday screamed. "I was fuckin' tortured for days until you fuckin' showed up! What do we have now?! We've got nothing!"

"A hard past is not an excuse being a fucking piece of shit in the present," Barcomb said. "Ash has always had your fuckin' back and you fuckin' shoot her so you can fuck off in a helicopter and die on some pretty little island all by yourself? Fuck that."

A single zombie came up onto the roof.

"If you're gonna kill yourself," Barcomb said, "fucking do it. I ain't gonna stop you. I always knew you were a fuckin' coward."

The zombie got closer and Barcomb saw its face.

"Fuck me," he said.

"No!" Munday screamed. "Not him!"

It was Duke McBride, his skin pale white, his eyes unfocused and his jaw hanging open. There was a large open wound below his chin, a great big hole with flaps of skin hanging off.

Duke seemed to look past Barcomb. Barcomb swore he could see a hint of recognition in his eyes when he locked onto Munday.

"No!" Munday screamed.

Barcomb scowled at her and stepped aside.

Munday screamed hysterically as Duke jumped onto her and clawed at her throat. His teeth sank into her skin and clamped down on her windpipe. She screamed and drowned in her own blood as Duke tore at her windpipe like a dog with a toy, shaking his head and freeing it from her neck.

Rachel Munday was thrown into a dark seizure from which she would never emerge. Every last ounce of energy in her body was expended in her violent convulsions. Every thought her brain would ever have again flashed through her head at lightning speed. She had no idea what was happening to her. She had only sensations of pain and thoughts of pain and then, when she had lost enough blood and couldn't get enough air, Rachel had nothing.

"Hey, Duke," Barcomb said.

Duke stood up with Munday's blood dripping from his lips. He growled at Barcomb.

"Thanks for the assist, asshole."

Barcomb kicked Duke hard in the chest and sent him toppling backwards off the rooftop to a second, much messier death below. His head popped on impact with the concrete.

Barcomb scowled at Munday's corpse. He rolled her off the rooftop too and watched her body splatter below.

A sounds started up. It was the six-wheeler truck.

Barcomb rushed over to the other side of the roof. Haws plowed the truck through a dozen zombies and parked it right in front of the gate. The numbers were thinning now. He looked down at the ground below for Ash. There was no sign of her.

"Ash!" Barcomb shouted.

Gunshots sounded behind him from inside the house. He ignored them.

"Ash!" he shouted again.

He looked around for her. He started looking at the faces of the zombies, praying she hadn't turned. She wouldn't want that. Suddenly, he heard something from behind him.

"You looking for me?"

Barcomb turned. Ash grabbed him and hugged him.

"Not too tight," Ash said, pulling back. "She nailed me right in the shoulder."

"I thought you were dead," Barcomb said.

"That seems to be going around," Ash replied with a smile.

"How did you-"

"I fucked up my leg pretty bad," she said, "but it wasn't so bad. I landed on a car, too. That was fun."

"You landed on a car?"

"It's still drivable."

Ash and Barcomb held each other and looked down at the yard. Haws got out of the truck and started picking off the few remaining zombies.

"What do you think about this place?" Barcomb asked.

"What about it?"

"Is it livable?"

Ash touched Barcomb's face and kissed him.

"Anywhere's livable," Ash said, smiling, "as long as we managed to stay the fuck alive."

"Damn fuckin' right," Barcomb said.

Chapter 10: No Place Like Home

Six months later, there was barely a trace of death within the walls of their new home. Barcomb, Haws and Ash had taken every corpse ten miles down the road on the back of a borrowed flat-bed truck and burned them in the middle of the afternoon. Munday was thrown in there with the others. She was given no special treatment. She was the same as any other corpse. Nobody got upset and claimed otherwise. She was thrown on the ground just the same and her decaying corpse burnt just the same, too. It took a long time to gather enough paint to repaint the walls, to get rid of all the pink stains, but they got there. After three months, they had picked their own rooms and settled down. Barcomb and Ash took the master bedroom. Haws liked it best in the basement, down with the equipment and the firearms. He took to working on the Humvee most days, to get her back to her best. He'd done it before and he'd do it again, that's what he kept saying. He was slower with one hand down for a while, but he was learning new tricks. The missing hand still tickled sometimes. Lauren, which they later learned was Pocahontas's real name, slept in the pantry. It took a while to get her to sleep anywhere but the kennels and to walk on two legs, but they got there. Barcomb sat with her for hours every day, talking to her about the world, about the things he'd seen and done before the world changed forever. He talked only about the good things, about fishing trips and birthday parties, game days and fight nights. At first, he did it only for her benefit, but he came to enjoy it. The house on the side of the hill had seen a lot of horror, but slowly, like the fading tide, that horror subsided and was replaced with something else. The walls kept them safe from the outside world. It took longer for them all to feel safe from their thoughts and memories. They spent long nights sat up drinking and talking about all the things that they'd seen and done. They could repaint the walls, but they could never cover over the mental

233

scars the end of the world had given them. But that was OK, Barcomb thought. They were lucky.

To be alive was to be lucky, that was Barcomb's conclusion.

It was a Saturday in November when Barcomb woke up with the sun shining through the curtains and felt beside him and discovered that Ash had already gotten up. He checked the bathroom. She wasn't there. The morning sickness was getting to her recently. The idea of bringing a baby into this world didn't sit well with Barcomb, but maybe that's what the world needed, he thought. They made the decision together. They carefully plotted out all of the supplies they'd need, all the supplies they had, and the reliability of the house's defenses. They judged the odds of their deaths. They accounted for everything: zombies, raiders, the military, animals, everything. Nothing was getting through their walls. Nothing was getting into their house. Nothing was getting into their lives. They had complete control.

Barcomb sometimes felt it was too good to be true.

He slipped on some pants and walked out of the bedroom. The sound of static reverberated throughout the house. Confused, Barcomb wandered down the hallway and looked down at the lounge from the balcony. The TV was on.

Static.

Barcomb walked down the stairs and turned it off. He still heard it.

Static.

The radio was on.

234

"What the fuck?" Barcomb said. He walked over to the radio and turned it off. "Ash?" he called.

A faint hissing sound came from the door to the basement. Barcomb opened the door and walked down, his bare feet slapping on the tiled floor along the way. He scratched the back of his neck. It was the only pain he could get rid of easily. His battle scars - the bullet wounds, the stab wounds, the broken bones, everything - they ached and burned and itched alternately. The cold made some worse; the heat bothered the rest. It took him a while to come to terms with it, to be anything other than constantly irritated. Walking down the steps into the basement, his knee was shot with sharp pain with each step.

"Haws, man," Barcomb said. "You down here?"

The hissing grew louder with each step. Barcomb reached the bottom and the static was all around, from every car radio and ham radio in the room, about a dozen in all. Haws and Ash were crowded around the long distance radio. They both turned and looked at him at the same time.

"What the fuck is going on?" Barcomb said. "Turn off some of these fuckin' radios, for fuck's sake. What are you even doing?"

Neither Haws nor Ash spoke.

Barcomb shrugged. "What?" he said. "What is it?"

"The radios all started up about ten minutes ago," Ash said.

"Something big is going down," Haws said.

"We heard someone speaking," Ash said. "It sounded like an emergency broadcast. It came through on every radio."

"Must've been automatically triggered by something," Barcomb said. "There's can't be anyone left to broadcast anything like this."

They listened to the static. They listened long enough until the hissing started to form patterns. They listened a little longer until they heard the words.

"Two minutes..." it said.

"imp..." it said.

They all looked at each other. It went back to static again.

"Imp?" Haws said.

"Imp?" Barcomb parroted. "Gimp?"

"Why would someone be on the radio talking about gimps?" Ash said, raising an eyebrow and folding her arms.

"Implosion?" Haws said.

"Fuck," Barcomb said.

The radio spoke again. "Imp..." it said. "One..."

"Impact," Barcomb said.

"What..." Ash said.

"The roof!" Barcomb said. "Right now!"

"Maybe we should stay-" Ash said.

Barcomb and Haws were already running up the stairs.

"What do you think it is?" Haws shouted as they ran.

Ash followed.

They ran out onto the roof, past the helicopter, and stopped at the edge. They looked around and were silent for a moment. Over the valley and the hills in the distance they could see Elizabeth. There were a few small towns dotted around. Beyond all that lay Jersey City and the skyscrapers of New York City. The fires had long since died out. From a distance, it even looked calm. Haws chuckled.

"Well," Haws asked, "what the fuck is this all about?"

"I don't know," Barcomb answered.

"I don't see anything," Ash said. "What do you think the range is on that radio? Maybe it's from another state. We don't know what the hell is going on."

Barcomb touched Ash on the back to calm her. "It's OK. False alarm," Barcomb said. "I thought maybe it was the military, something like that. Must be some kind of echo."

"Echo?" Haws said. "Fuck you talking about, an echo?"

Barcomb shrugged. He took a deep breath and kissed Ash.

"I'm sorry," he said, putting his arm around her. Barcomb laughed. "Didn't mean to panic you. It's just some weird shit is all."

Barcomb stood with his arm around Ash, looking out across the state. He placed a hand on her stomach and smiled at her. Haws looked at them and grinned. "Look at you two," he said. "Happy as pigs in shit."

Barcomb and Ash laughed.

Slowly, their moment of peace became something else. It began first as a low rumble. They barely heard it at first. It didn't even register. When Barcomb first noticed it, he wasn't worried.

Generator, he thought. Must be working overtime.

It was cold, but it was a beautiful morning.

The rumbling grew louder and louder. It began to trouble Barcomb. He looked around. He looked at Ash. It was troubling her, too.

"What's that noise?" Haws said.

Barcomb looked up at the sky. He didn't see any planes, just clouds, clouds a thin white arched line.

"What…" Barcomb said.

Ash saw it, too. "What is it?" she said.

"We better…" Barcomb said. "We should probably…"

The arched white line was growing in the sky. It was looping down. It was getting faster as it got closer to the ground. Barcomb didn't know exactly what it was, but his stomach seemed to know. There was a wrenching sickness coming on as the pit in his stomach grew larger and deeper. Every ounce of hope he had felt only moments earlier faded as the arched white cloud reached down towards the earth.

It reached down to New York City.

The sky lit up in a blinding white flash.

Barcomb, Ash and Haws covered their eyes.

When they opened their eyes, New York City was gone, replaced with a mushroom cloud reaching up into the sky. They could see a searing wall of fire crossing the state. Elizabeth's tallest buildings collapsed under the weight of a dust cloud a mile high. The dust cloud kept coming, flattening trees, throwing cars and small buildings into the air.

"Into the basement!" Barcomb shouted. "Now!"

Barcomb pulled Ash into the house and down the stairs. Haws was close behind them, closing every door. "I'll get Lauren!" he shouted, turning off as Barcomb and Ash went for the basement.

"What the fuck was that?" Ash said. "What the fuck?!"

Barcomb shut the basement door and ran down the stairs to hold Ash in his arms. He wiped away her tears. "It's OK," he said. "It's OK."

"Shut the fuck up," Ash mumbled. "It's not OK, is it?"

Barcomb looked at her. He could hardly bear to say it, but he felt it in his heart. Haws and Lauren ran into the basement and slammed the door behind them.

"What the fuck is going on?" Haws shouted.

Barcomb looked at him and said, "It was a nuclear bomb. They've wiped New York City off the map."

"Why the fuck would they do that?!" Haws asked.

"It must be a control measure," Barcomb replied. "Things must be out of control. Things must be worse than we thought."

Barcomb touch Ash's face and made her look at him through her tears. "Ash," he said. "You're right. It's not OK. Nothing is OK.

Barcomb took Ash's hand.

He kissed her and said, "Things will never be the same again."

TO BE CONTINUED...

Made in the USA
Las Vegas, NV
28 September 2021